DAGNEY SKULLY
AND THE PENDULUM BEAD STRINGS

DAGNEY SKULLY
AND THE PENDULUM BEAD STRINGS

SARENA SCHUMACHER

TINY DOG PRESS

This is a work of fiction. Names, characters, organizations, places, events, and incidents are either products of the author's imagination or are used fictitiously.

Published by Tiny Dog Press, Friday Harbor
www.DagneySkully.com

Edited and Designed by Girl Friday Productions
www.girlfridayproductions.com
Editorial: Clete Smith, Lynn Post, Rachelle Longé McGhee
Design: Paul Barrett
Illustrations: Sarena Schumacher

ISBN (Paperback): 978-1-7336095-0-0
e-ISBN: 978-1-7336095-1-7

First Edition

Printed in the United States of America

Home is always the best place to be,
even if it happens to be in an outhouse.

—Dagney Skully

This book is dedicated to all of humannity.

CHAPTER 1

WELL, WAIL, WHALE

Although he wasn't a camper, Harold Pew hustled into the Shaw County Park campground outhouse and latched the door behind him. It was not his first time inside this outhouse. His forty-five-acre property on Shaw Island bordered the park, so he often walked through the campground to get to the beach. He spent plenty of time there and used the outhouse regularly.

As he entered the wooden structure, he noticed a new cabinet had been installed on the back wall. The cabinet was shallow, only an inch deep. Harold's curiosity got the best of him, so he cautiously opened the cabinet door. To his delight, he found three rows of bead strings hanging within. They were about six inches long, each consisting of a dazzling pattern of alternating bead colors and sizes: purple and yellow, with a hint of azure blue, or chartreuse green on bright pink, with a subtle hint of magenta. The colors and patterns were limitless, each one unique to itself. Strung in the middle of each pattern were four square beads, each consisting of one letter. The four-letter combination spelled a word. Harold looked over all the bead strings and read each word. They all appeared to be unrelated to one another; just one random four-letter word on each string. Above the top row of bead strings was a handwritten note tacked to the wall. It read,

Bead strings made by Dagney Skully. Take one.

There were fourteen to choose from. He chose one with the word "MUCK."

Strange, he thought. *What's it supposed to mean?* But he liked the colors of the beads and he liked the random word, so he took it. He put it in his pocket and as he did, a surge of energy overcame him, filling him with love, respect, and appreciation for all of life and all things good. Feeling renewed, he carried on with his business.

As Harold turned to leave, he noticed a wooden box about two feet tall by two feet wide tucked in the front corner of the outhouse. It was not fancy, nor was it painted. An arched door about eight inches tall was situated in the middle of the box. A sign that read "The Skullys" hung crooked above the door, and a tiny welcome mat lay at the threshold.

That must be where Dagney Skully lives, thought Harold. Hoping to meet his new neighbors and the maker of the bead strings, he kneeled down and tapped on the door. Moments later the door opened. A man, no taller than a toothbrush, stood in the doorway; behind him, a young girl.

"Are you the Skullys?" asked Harold.

"Yes, sir," Mr. Skully replied. "I am Cecil Skully, and this is my daughter, Dagney."

"I found your bead strings, Dagney. I love them! I took this one." He held it down for Dagney to see.

"You got the first one!" said Dagney.

"They're amazing; thanks, Dagney! I'm Harold, Harold Pew." He reached out to shake Dagney's hand. "We're neighbors. I live on the property next to the campground."

"Nice to meet you, Harold," said Dagney.

"Nice to meet you too, Cecil Skully," said Harold as he shook the small man's hand. "Your little condo here is new. I've never seen it before," he added.

"It was built just for me and my family. My pops accepted a job working at the campground, and they promised us free housing. We moved in two days ago. There's a kitchen, a big living room, a den, and our own bathroom," said Dagney. "Everything we need, right in here!"

"No bedrooms? Where do you sleep?" asked Harold.

"Muter sleeps in the kitchen, usually. Pops sleeps in the bathroom. Corey, my oldest brother, sleeps in the living room, and I sleep in the closet with my baby brother, Marlin.

"Are you comfortable?" asked Harold.

"Very! We even have a telephone and hot water. Ranger Kate picks up our mail at the post office and helps us out in any other way we need," answered Dagney.

"Fantastic! Welcome to Shaw Island. Let me know if you need anything. By the way, there is a Free Pile up the road. You can cut through my pasture to get there," said Harold.

Moments after Harold uttered the words "Free Pile," a woman, no taller than a pencil, appeared in the doorway.

"Did you say 'Free Pile'?" asked the woman.

"Yes, there is a kiosk up the street at the community center. Free items available for everyone. Take the shortcut through my pasture," said Harold.

"Edna Skully," she said as she shoved Mr. Skully aside to greet her new neighbor.

"You must be Dagney's mother?" asked Harold.

"I am. When is the Free Pile open?" asked Edna.

"Day and night. Always open," answered Harold.

"Thank you, neighbor," said Edna.

"Of course," said Harold, and he put his bead string back in his pocket.

Mrs. Skully was already getting herself together for a trip to the Free Pile, as Mr. Skully and Dagney went back inside and shut the front door.

Friendly folks, thought Harold as he exited the outhouse. *I hope they stick around awhile.* He carried on down to the beach as he felt the wonderful energy of his new bead string.

* * *

Shaw County Park campground was situated on a little island off the far northwest corner of the United States. After a year of unemployment, Pops had been offered a position at the park. These were hard times. Jobs were scarce and money was slim, so he accepted the job and they moved into the outhouse condo, in the beautiful San Juan Islands, surrounded by the Salish Sea. It was magical.

The five members of the Skully family arrived on Shaw Island early one spring after traveling across the country from New Jersey in the family wagon.

The outhouse was magnificent! The solid wood structure, with gabled roof, concrete floor, and big, sturdy door, was cleaned daily by Park Ranger Kate. A few steps led up to the door, which had two holes in the bottom, drilled out for members of the Skully family to pass through. Once inside the outhouse, they could find comfort in the small condo that was designed and built just for them.

The Shaw Island County campground stretched about a quarter of a mile along the upper embankment of the long, sandy beach. Facing south, it captured the sun from dawn to dusk. It was a small campground, with only eleven campsites, and every camper who visited the Skullys' outhouse came out forever changed. No one could resist the temptation of opening the shallow cabinet to see what was stored inside. As each person chose their bead string, a surge of energy enveloped them, which gave them respect and appreciation for all of life and all things good.

* * *

Years back, Pops had inherited a grandfather clock. Before Grandmother died, she had told him, "The clock hasn't worked in ages, but when it did, it had a phenomenal power. Hard to describe, but the continuous motion of the pendulum created an energy that caused great things to happen. Then one day the clock broke, and most of the energy fizzled out. That's when I put it into storage. It's been there for many years. I hope you can get it working again. It will bring magic, of a sort, into your life."

Pops liked the clock for sentimental reasons alone, so he was determined to get it running again. "I'm gonna get that clock working tomorrow," Pops would say every day after work. Then he would pick up his banjo and pick at it for the next three hours before falling asleep in the bathroom.

* * *

In her earlier years, Muter had won a lifetime supply of pickled herring by placing second in a beauty contest. She loved starting her day with four cups of hot coffee, pickled herring, and a bagel with lox. She figured she should leave some out for the rest of her family as well. Her cooking skills were poor and she didn't like to clean either. Instead, she scattered flour on the floor to disguise the dirt. They were all sloppy eaters, so Marlin's meals consisted of herring that had fallen to the floor and handfuls of flour.

Pops loved his morning coffee too. He would finish his third cup while reading excerpts from the *Shaw Island Daily Journal*, reciting headlines such as: **RICHEST MAN ON EARTH LIVES ON SHAW ISLAND**

and **MAYOR APPROVES CONDOMINIUM DEVELOPMENT, LOCATION NOT YET ESTABLISHED.** Pops loved reading the news to his family. It made him feel smart. He was a simple farmer from the Midwest who never got past the eighth grade, but he loved his wife and children and always did what was best for the family.

After moving into the outhouse, Dagney took an interest in the grandfather clock. "I'm going to get this clock working, Pops," she said as they moved it into its new location in the outhouse condo.

The interior mechanics of the clock, along with the motionless pendulum, fascinated her. When she opened the back to gain access to the working "guts" of the clock, she discovered a small wooden box lying on the bottom. Opening the lid, she found it stocked full of colorful beads. Some were tiny seed beads, others were a bit larger, and some had letters imprinted on them. Engraved on the underside of the lid was a poem. Dagney read it.

> Thus, string the beads with letters four
> The words you spell will ever more
> Protect you from what danger lies
> Below, above, before your eyes.
>
> And all who wear the string of bead
> Good fortune come through others' deed
> Of kindness, love, and forward pay
> Their actions shall be your same way.

There was a spot for a third stanza to the poem. It remained empty.

Delighted with her find, Dagney's attention turned from clock repair to bead strings. She loved combining different colors, and even more, loved making up the words. She stuck to the rule of the poem and only used four-letter words. After making hundreds of them, she one day realized that no matter how many bead strings she made, she never ran out of beads. She had several theories as to how this was possible. Marlin listened to her theories as he crawled around on the floor, looking for scraps of herring. Some were silly, some were non-sense, but some were so brilliant, they might possibly be true.

"My first theory," said Dagney, "is that the beads don't really exist."

Marlin looked confused. The beads most certainly did exist.

"That's right, Marlin," she went on, "nothing really exists. You and I do not exist, but since I am, in fact, here, that means that I am a figment of my own nonexistent imagination. If that is true, then the beads that don't exist actually do exist in my nonexistent imagina-tion. Therefore, I always have beads because I am always imagining them . . . theoretically."

Marlin threw a spoon. He didn't like that theory because it made no sense.

"Theory number two," said Dagney, "is that—like sands through the hourglass—so are the beads in this box."

Marlin knew that there were countless grains of sand in an hour-glass, but grains of sand are much smaller than the beads, so it didn't add up. He demanded more theories.

"Ok, Marlin," she continued, "I think Pops fills the bead box when I'm asleep, and I hate to spoil it for you, but I'm pretty sure Pops is the tooth fairy too."

From the other room, Pops hollered out, "Dagney, stop telling your brother those lies!"

As Dagney strung her beads, she lowered her voice and whispered, "Marlin, I think the truth is, the bead box was originally empty except for the bead singularity. The *bead singularity* is when all the beads that could ever possibly exist are compressed down into nothing. When the grandfather clock originally started ticking, it caused the 'bead bang' and every bead that ever existed within is now expanding outward infinitely. Like the stars in the universe itself, I will never run out of beads."

It was that brilliant theory that captured Marlin's attention and encouraged his interest in science, so Dagney started reading him science books about the universe. Stephen Hawking's *The Theory of Everything: The Origin and Fate of the Universe* was their favorite. They learned about galaxies, wormholes, and time travel. Dagney loved these books too and thought that someday she could write about her bead-string theories.

Marlin loved the bead strings, so Dagney pinned one to his diaper. His bead-string word was "KELP." It was a bit like a tail, which pleased Marlin so much that, were it actually a tail, it would always be wagging. Instead, it dragged behind, collecting flour and sand and whatever else he crawled through. On this particular day, it was collecting dried grass clippings. He crawled his way through the grassy field to play on the bright-orange and lime-green kayaks left by some campers. Bright orange and lime green are hard colors to ignore when you're Marlin's age, especially when you can crawl into the cockpit and way up into the bow. And that is exactly what he did. While playing inside the bow of the kayak, the owners returned to go for a paddle. The boat was lifted up, carried a short distance, and then dropped. It made a splash as the bow was set into the water. The stern scraped the sand as it was pushed out farther into the bay. Then the boat became entirely buoyant. Marlin could not have been more thrilled as the camper entered the cockpit and shoved her feet up toward him. The sound of water sloshing against the hull and the bobbing sensation of the kayak as it headed away from shore were soothing and quickly lulled Marlin to sleep. It was a wonderful sleep. A long, deep, peaceful sleep like he had never experienced before.

THUD! AAAAAAHHHHHH!

A jarring collision of the kayak, followed by a loud shriek, woke Marlin. It was an unpleasant way to end his peaceful slumber. He could hear loud splashes, like the sound of his fat uncle doing a belly flop in the deep end of the pool. The kayaker's feet began flailing, and the paddling became quick and erratic. And then another THUD!— this time even louder, right on the side of the hull where Marlin was lying. It hit so hard, it lifted the boat up and out of the water, tilting it sideways. The kayaker wailed in terror as the boat capsized. In an instant, the kayaker fell out, and water came rushing in. It quickly filled the entire hull of the kayak. Although there was not much Marlin could do, he had the instinct to swim out of the cockpit, and as he did, he caught a glimpse of the largest fish he'd seen in his life. It was black and white, like a zebra, except more spotted than striped.

He remembered Pops had talked about a big black-and-white spotted fish that swam out in the Salish Sea, except Pops had called them "wells." "When they came to the surface," Pops had said, "they would exhale, and it looked like they were shooting out water." Marlin knew what a *well* was; he had seen one before at his uncle's house out in the desert. So he had an image of what the black-and-white fish looked like when they were shooting out water. These wells were black and white for sure, but not at all how Marlin had imagined. They were far more amazing. Their dolphinlike bodies spanned the length of a school bus, and a tall fin, shaped like half a surfboard, stuck upward from the middle of their backs. Sharp, spiky teeth lined up perfectly around the perimeter of their gaping mouths. The wells were hunting and feeding on Chinook salmon. One would share with another as they ripped a fish in half. There were fish and fins and tails and bubbles right above Marlin. But as he observed this pod of feeding wells, he sank deeper and deeper. The brilliant glow of the sun turned to darkness as he continued his downward journey. He sank to the bottom of the Salish Sea, bead string in tow.

By now Pops had returned home from work. He walked in the house, looked at the clock and said, "Tomorrow, I'm going to get that clock working again." Then he picked up his banjo and started to play. Suddenly it occurred to him that he had not seen Marlin. "Where is the boy, Muter?" But he didn't wait for an answer. He dropped his banjo, ran out of the condo, wriggled through the hole in the door of the outhouse, and ran down the campground road, calling out, "Marlin, Marlin. . . ." He ran through the grassy field where the kayaks had been sitting, and on down to the sandy beach. "Marlin . . . Marlin . . . ,"

he yelled, hoping to see his young son in droopy diapers. No sight of Marlin anywhere. In a panic, he kept running. As he approached the far end of the beach, where the sand turned to large rocky outcroppings, Pops spotted a head emerging from the water. Then came the body. Then the soggy diaper. Sitting on top of a rock crab, Marlin was escorted ashore, bead string still trailing behind.

This amazing rescue is how the magic of the bead string worked. Because this particular day happened to be a full moon, the tidal currents were at their strongest. The pull of the tide, along with the drag of the bead string, had directed Marlin to land square on the back of Roy the Rock Crab, who had been waiting in line for entry into the food bank. Being a kind crab, he gave up his spot in line, to escort Marlin ashore. But the magic goes back further than that. So it was, just the day prior, Roy the Rock Crab had been combing through the eelgrass in shallow water, and since the tides were extreme that day, campers and dogs waded far out on the flat, sandy shoreline. When Roy suddenly found himself in the mouth of a dog, he reached up and pinched the dog hard on the nose. The dog yelped and tossed Roy onto dry sand, where he landed upside down, legs flailing in the air. The dog ran off with a bloody nose, leaving Roy completely immobilized in the receding tide. Roy was stuck. Beginning to feel the heat of the midsummer sun, he soon stopped flailing. It wouldn't be long before he ran out of oxygen. He longed for the coolness of the salty water, but he could do nothing. As he faded in and out of consciousness, a shade of bright lime green suddenly appeared beside him.

The next thing he knew he was upright in the hands of a woman who had just come ashore in her kayak. She held him up to her face and said, "My bead-string word is 'CRAB.' It's your lucky day." And with that, she gently placed Roy back in the cool Salish Sea, among the eelgrass, where he regained strength and returned to deeper, safer territory. Roy knew he must return a favor to someone, somewhere. He knew he must "pay it forward." And so it was, Roy returned Marlin to his family.

Pops thanked Roy the Rock Crab, grabbed Marlin, and carried him back to the outhouse, while the kayaker swam ashore safely.

CHAPTER 2

SCIENCE AND MUD

Muter was not much of an outdoor person. She fretted over natural disasters, such as a bird pooping on her head or stumbling into a mud puddle. Worse yet, she could trip in the pasture and land in horse manure, although somehow it didn't bother her that she was already living in an outhouse. She always avoided the outside world, except when it came to the Free Pile. Every day around ten a.m., Muter would hang up the phone, put on her muck boots, and journey through Harold's horse pasture. She would risk all the dangerous elements of the outside world to make the daily trip to this handy stash of free goods. It was a "take whatever you want buffet" of amazing items, both useful and fun. She brought home all kinds of treasures: a rolling pin, toys, books, a toilet plunger, pots, pans, and household tchotchkes that she loved to clutter the house up with.

It was a Saturday, so Pops was working a half-day shift. Dagney had gone out to work on her latest invention, the spring catapult. Potential energy, she thought, was a great medium to work with. On a bow and arrow, for example, when the string of a bow is pulled back, it contains potential energy. When the string is released, the potential energy turns into kinetic energy as the arrow is thrust toward its target. Dagney had found a spring from an old playground toy and rolled it up the hill to where the park meets the main road. She re-coiled the big, thick spring, using the block-and-tackle pulley method, to make it as tight as possible—the tighter the spring, the more potential energy it had—until it was tight enough that, with a quick sever of the rope, she could propel objects to the very tops of the trees. She fancied herself to be an inventor in this way, and practiced throughout the morning.

With her muck boots on and bag over her shoulder, Muter couldn't wait to see what she would find at the Free Pile that day. Other than campfire smoke, the air was always fresh when she came out of the outhouse. She stumbled her way through the woods, over twigs, logs, and branches, before coming to the clearing where Harold's pasture began. It was lumpy, bumpy, sloppy terrain, but it was a shortcut, so she always took that route. It was worth the risk, to get to the Free Pile faster.

When Muter was about halfway across the pasture, Dagney was re-coiling the spring in preparation for her next shot. She then placed an open can of refried beans, which someone had left behind at Campsite #8, on the platform of the lever. She would soon discover how the twelve-ounce can would react as the potential energy turned into kinetic energy. The goal was distance. Everything was in place—spring, tension, knife, beans—now all she had to do was release the spring. She placed her pocketknife on the rope, then sliced through it briskly. As the rope cut, the spring released, hurling the can far off into the distance, above the alder trees. Dagney had no particular target; she just wanted to see how far it could go. It went far! As the can flew way out over the alder thicket, she was pleased to see bean chunks flinging from it. This was her farthest shot yet. Now she needed to work on her aim.

Harold Pew had just returned home from the feed store, where he'd purchased bails of timothy hay. His horses were quite hungry and waiting patiently for their meal. As Muter cautiously made her way through the pasture, she had one thing on her mind: a treasure trove of goodies awaiting her at the Free Pile! As she hurried through the bumpy field, a chunk of beans suddenly landed directly on top of her head. Just as she always feared, she thought a bird had pooped on her. The beans oozed down her face and into her eye sockets. Blindly, she hustled toward the horse trough to rinse off. In doing so, she ran directly into a puddle of thick, mucky mud where the pond was drying up. This was Muter's worst nightmare. The mud was like quicksand, and she was sinking. One cannot swim in a thick puddle of mucky mud, but Muter still tried. Despite her best efforts, she just couldn't stay afloat. Her first thought was, *What will I miss at the Free Pile today?* She still couldn't see with the "bird poop" in her eyes, and she was now shoulder-deep in the muck. Completely helpless, it looked like the end of Muter.

Just then, Harold came calling for his horses. As he scanned the pasture, a graceful, gliding movement from across the field caught his eye. *That's peculiar,* he thought and walked across the pasture to investigate the mysterious flying object. It landed near the drying pond. As he approached, he realized it was a Frisbee. When he bent over to pick it up, he noticed Muter, covered in beans down to her neck and sinking in mud up to her shoulders. He remembered the word "MUCK" on the bead string he had acquired on his recent visit to the campground outhouse, and he knew right away that it could help save Muter from the puddle. "Hang on, Edna, I can help you!" he assured her as he pulled the bead string from his pocket and tossed it out to her.

"Grab ahold, Edna," he commanded. "Grab the bead string; I'll pull you out!"

It took several attempts. Although Muter couldn't see, she finally grabbed ahold, and Harold pulled Muter out of her muddy grave. She would live another day to acquire more treasures from the Free Pile.

"Thank you, Harold. What a nightmare!" said Muter.

"Lucky I saw you! If it wasn't for this Frisbee that came gliding out of nowhere, I would not have seen you at all!" replied Harold as he led Muter to the horse trough to wash off.

The Frisbee had been Dagney's very next catapult shot. She had quickly re-coiled the spring, loaded the Frisbee onto the platform, and sliced the rope. The Frisbee sailed through the air, wobbly at first, but then caught a strong updraft and leveled out. It flew in the same general direction as the can of beans and disappeared over the alder grove into the adjacent pasture.

By the time Harold had Muter pulled from the muck, Dagney had made her way up the road, past the alders to see where her catapult shots had landed. She arrived just in time to see her neighbor helping Muter rinse the beans from her eyes. In Harold's hand, Dagney saw the Frisbee she'd just sent gliding. After seeing the trouble she'd created, she quietly slipped away, back into the alder thicket.

The whole next week, Dagney worked on distance and accuracy, with various objects of differing weight, and for the rest of his life, Harold wondered where that lifesaving Frisbee had come from.

CHAPTER 3

THE BIRDS AND THE BEES

Up the road from the Skullys' outhouse (Outhouse #2) was another outhouse: Outhouse #1. Marlin had not yet been to Outhouse #1, but he'd heard it housed a library. Dagney had just finished reading him the famous space scientist Michio Kaku's book *Beyond Einstein: The Cosmic Quest for the Theory of the Universe*, so now he was ready to learn about "antigravity technology." Hoping to find a book on the subject, Marlin made his first visit to Outhouse #1.

He was disappointed to see that the "library" was just a magazine rack. He "thumbed through" the stack of magazines: *People, Better Homes and Gardens, Reader's Digest*, and *National Geographic*. Marlin pulled out the *Nat Geo*, rolled it up, and pushed it like a log down the dusty campground road, back toward his own Outhouse #2.

It was August, so the days were long. The sun was high in the sky, and temperatures would be soaring into the nineties. It hadn't rained in forty-three days. The campground was full, which meant all eleven campsites were occupied. Families with children rode bicycles, went beachcombing, walked their dogs, and played Frisbee in the grass. Dagney was as busy as ever replenishing her bead-string cabinet. It ran out as quickly as she restocked it. String after string, each camper became a new member of the bead-string culture. Because of this, random good deeds and acts of kindness were happening everywhere. It had a snowball effect; whenever someone performed a random act of kindness, their bead-string power was elevated. They could physically feel the effects of their "good deeds" throughout their whole body. Amazing things continued to happen. Dagney's work was beneficial to everyone, and no one was denied a bead string.

Muter, as she did every day, had gone to the Free Pile. Pops was busy bundling firewood, and Dagney was practicing her catapult skills down by the boat ramp. By now she had mastered accuracy with various weights, distances, and speed of re-coil. The campers were all busy with their vacation activities. Some of the more curious ones went off to explore the island's monastery, Our Lady of the Rock, which was located somewhere in the middle of the island.

The monastery was run by Benedictine nuns who wore the traditional black-and-white garb, called a "habit," and sustained themselves by growing their own food and raising livestock. They raised Highland cattle, sheep, chickens, llamas, and ostriches. The largest of the flightless birds, ostriches were raised as working animals to help out around the farm by pulling carts, which were usually loaded with hay or vegetables. The nuns were an important part of Shaw Island.

Periodically, the liveliest nun, Sister Hilda, would stroll through the park just to get out and about.

As Marlin rolled his magazine log down the campground road, his bead string dragging behind in the dust, he passed by the only faucet in the campground. It delivered great-tasting drinkable water that animals and humans alike depended on. Since it hadn't rained in quite a long time, the ponds and puddles had all dried up. Because the campground was at full capacity, the water faucet was in regular use and a puddle of fresh water had accumulated below the spigot. Birds of all kinds used this as an opportunity to bathe and drink: wrens, chickadees, woodpeckers, and of course those pesky crows that steal food from picnic tables the moment you walk away. Word got out quickly in the bird community about this available source of fresh water.

High above the campground, a bald eagle circled. He had his eye on the puddle and was getting ready to land for a drink of fresh water. Upon his descent, the eagle suddenly noticed Marlin, who looked like a large mouse. Changing his mind about the water, he decided in favor of a tasty noontime snack. Positioning himself in alignment with the campground road, like a plane coming in for landing, the eagle swooped down, grabbed Marlin by the diaper, and in one continuous motion ascended into the sky. Off he flew, back toward his nest, to enjoy his freshly caught snack.

From down the road at the boat ramp, Dagney witnessed Marlin's abduction. Horrified, she knew she had to do something. Her brother's life was in extreme danger. *Why is Marlin always getting himself into trouble like this? Someone really needs to keep a better eye on him,* she thought. In a panic, she looked around to see if anyone could help. All the campers were so busy enjoying the sun and the sandy beach, that no one had noticed the tragic event. Dagney fell to her knees in despair. When she looked up, she saw Sister Hilda with her cart-pulling ostrich come strolling down the dusty park road. This was a younger ostrich that she had lovingly named Rose Buddy and was training to pull carts.

"I need your ostrich. How much does she weigh?" asked Dagney, as she ran up to Sister Hilda.

"She weighs two hundred and fifteen pounds, but she is not for sale," Sister Hilda readily answered.

"I don't want to buy her; I just need to borrow her." And with that, Dagney hastily removed the harness from the ostrich. This annoyed the sister to a great extent.

"I beg your pardon!" exclaimed Sister Hilda as she grabbed the ostrich back from Dagney.

Dagney pulled at the ostrich as she tried to explain her emergency. "The eagle . . . he's . . . Marlin . . . he's got Marlin . . . ," Dagney stammered.

Sister pulled back on her ostrich. She had only known the Skullys for a short time and had thought they were nice, friendly neighbors. Dagney's behavior made Sister Hilda now think otherwise. "This is absurd! Let go of my ostrich, you little hoodlum!" she exclaimed.

By this time, the eagle was halfway back to his nest, which was two hundred feet up a tree, some three hundred yards down the shoreline. Marlin loved the view from up high, but he did not much care for the tight grip of the eagle's talon. He was going to give that eagle a good "talking to."

Ranger Kate had just started restocking magazines in Outhouse #1 when she heard the squabble. She ran to see what the trouble was. Pops heard the commotion too and came running just in time to find Sister Hilda and Dagney in a tug-of-war with an ostrich. As Ranger Kate tried to make sense of what had happened, Dagney ran to Outhouse #2, opened the bead-string cabinet, and grabbed one with the word "BIRD."

"Sister, take this bead string as collateral for your ostrich," Dagney begged. "She will be returned, I promise," Dagney assured her. Reluctantly, Sister Hilda handed over her ostrich and watched as Dagney and Pops ran back to the boat ramp with Rose Buddy. Although Sister Hilda watched in disbelief, she was now part of the bead-string culture, and she felt it. She felt the magnificent energy the bead string delivered throughout her body. The love, respect, and appreciation for all of life and all things good overpowered her concern for Rose Buddy. She could now see the value of life in all things, even those pesky crows that always tried to steal the shiny parts from her broken-down Volkswagen Bug.

By now the eagle had landed. As he rested on the edge of his nest, Marlin reached up and slapped him right on the side of his beak. The eagle had never been slapped by his food before; it was a jolting surprise! Just as he was about to slap back—PLOP!—an ostrich landed right in the middle of his nest. "Greetings, my name is Rose Buddy," said the ostrich. The eagle nearly fell out of his nest as he swooned at the magnificence of Rose Buddy's glossy plumage.

"Robin . . . I mean eagle . . . err, uhh . . . I mean Robin. I'm an eagle. My name is Robin," stammered Robin the Eagle.

Rose Buddy batted her eyelashes at Robin while explaining that she had been sent on a mission to save Marlin. She was very good at communicating with other birds. Robin the Eagle instantly fell deeply in love with Rose Buddy. Lovesick, he immediately handed Marlin over to his new love. The ostrich then called out to her best friend, Rumble. Rumble was a bumblebee. He was the biggest, fattest, fuzziest bumblebee on Shaw Island. Rumble was not only the biggest, but he was the kindest too, and always willing to lend a helping hand. Rose Buddy was also very good at communicating with bees, and Rumble came flying to Rose Buddy as soon as he heard her. She introduced Robin the Eagle and Marlin to Rumble.

"How do you do?" said Robin.

"How do you do?" said Rumble.

"How do you do?" said Marlin.

As they all formally greeted each other, Rose Buddy swooned and ruffled her feathers for Robin the Eagle. She was quite smitten herself.

While the two birds exchanged flirtatious feather fluffing, Rumble grabbed Marlin and brought him gently down into a patch of bright-pink coneflower. Rumble loved coneflower, and Marlin loved being back on ground level. Having witnessed the miraculous rescue, Pops and Dagney ran to the coneflower patch, thankful that Marlin was safe. Marlin cuddled Rumble and they became fast friends. Pops invited Rumble to stay for dinner that night.

Rumble was a longtime resident of Shaw Island, and he had many friends. Three of his friends came for dinner at the Skullys'

that night too: Kaos the Ladybug, Sparks the Firefly, and Pokkitt the Preying Mantis. After dining on cabbage salad and baba ghanoush, they circled around the campfire, told stories, and roasted marshmallows. As the evening wore on, Pokkitt invited Dagney to go for a walk around the campground. Pokkitt was charming and friendly and told Dagney all about his interests and hobbies. He had been a self-made businessman in a faraway country, and he liked to knit. He offered to teach Dagney the art of the knitting needle. She offered to teach him the art of the bead string. They both accepted. Dagney was glad to have a new friend.

As they strolled back toward the outhouse, Pokkitt asked Dagney many questions about her life and her family. "What brought you to Outhouse #2?" he inquired.

"My pops found work here. He had a hard time getting work back in Jersey, so we came out here to the campground."

"It's a lovely place. Do you plan on staying long?" asked Pokkitt.

"I hope so," said Dagney. "We love it here, and we are fixing up the outhouse."

"That's very interesting, Dagney," said Pokkitt, stopping just outside the outhouse. "I need to be getting home now. But I feel I should warn you, Dagney. Do you see the hole in the base of that tree?" He pointed to the tree behind the staircase.

Dagney had to look hard, for it was well hidden with vegetation. "I think so," she said.

"Dagney, stay away from there. Stay away from that tree," Pokkitt implored. "There is poison ivy growing in and around there. Have you ever been stung by poison ivy, Dagney? It causes painful, itchy blisters. I once got the sap on my skin and had blisters all over my body for days. The pain was unbearable. So please, I'm warning you, stay away from that area. I don't want you to get blisters."

Dagney assured Pokkitt that she would stay away, and with that they each said "good night."

CHAPTER 4

FISHING FOR FANGTOOTH

The weeks of summer vacation had come to an end. Although the days were still long, and the skies were still blue, most of the campsites were now empty. The kids had gone back to school, leaving the older crowd to enjoy the quiet campground. Pops didn't have to work as hard keeping up with the supply of firewood, and Dagney had cut back on making bead strings as the occupancy of the campground dwindled.

As Muter brewed the second pot of coffee, Pops read headlines from the newspaper. **RICHEST MAN ON EARTH PICKS OUTHOUSE #2 LOCATION FOR CONDOMINIUM DEVELOPMENT**. Pops almost choked on his lox. "That's our outhouse!" he exclaimed. Pops was a pretty steady guy, but this threw him into a fit of anxiety.

Dagney had never seen him like this before. "What's wrong, Pops?"

"The richest man on Earth is going to build condominiums at Outhouse #2," Pops repeated. He was clearly upset.

"Why can't he build them at Outhouse #1?" asked Dagney.

Pops skimmed the article, muttering aloud, "Due to the current residents' hard work—"

Looking up at his family, he interjected, "Hey, that's us!" then continued reading. "The property value of Outhouse #2 is considerably higher than Outhouse #1. It has been chosen by Financial Headquarters to be the next site for the new condo development. Construction has been set to begin in six months."

Pops looked up at Muter as she stood frozen from the news. They stared at each other as Marlin ate handfuls of flour from the floor.

Dagney finished her coffee and herring. Since the bead cabinet was full, she had plenty of free time. Feeling somewhat concerned about her family's future, she packed up her fishing pole to go on an adventurous getaway. Recalling the pictures she had seen in Marlin's *National Geographic* magazine, she decided to go fishing for the extraordinary deep-sea fangtooth fish.

Fangtooth fish

With a fishing pole in one hand and her lunch bucket in the other, Dagney made her way through the woods and across the pasture, the same way Muter went to the Free Pile. Once she reached the main road, she stopped, set down her stuff, and stuck out her thumb. It is well known that when hitchhiking in the San Juan Islands, one will always get a safe and friendly ride. Sure enough, the first vehicle to come along stopped to pick her up. It was a dark-green 1947 Ford pickup truck with lots of rust throughout the body. The driver hoisted Dagney into the back of the truck, then handed her the bucket and pole.

It was one mile to the general store where the driver dropped her off. Dagney thanked the man and gave him a bead string with the word "FISH" on it. The driver smiled, tucked it in his shirt pocket, and got in line for the ferry. He was now part of the bead-string culture, and he could feel it. He felt the magnificent energy the bead string delivered throughout his body. He felt love, respect, and appreciation for all of life and all things good, even those pesky crows that always tore through the garbage in the back of his truck.

There was a small school and an even smaller library on Shaw Island, but no official town. The general store situated next to the ferry landing sold basic necessities, such as bagels, coffee, and matzo. Next to the general store stood the post office, and behind that, the marina, with a dozen or so small boats, including the Skullys' 1953 wooden boat. The particular fish Dagney hoped to catch required a voyage out of the safe, calm waters of the inner island passageways, into the open straits, where the bottom was deeper, the water was rougher, and the winds were stronger. If she wanted to catch the fangtooth fish, this is where she needed to go. She throttled up the engine and headed for the open sea.

Once she arrived, Dagney cast her line and waited. Off in the distance she could see a pod of orcas traveling south toward American Camp, a national historical park on San Juan Island. By now it was midafternoon, and the day wore vibrant shades of blue, green, and yellow. Freight barges passed by, carrying goods to and from China. A seal occasionally popped its head up to catch a breath and linger for a moment to see if Dagney was having any luck. She was surrounded by mountains and water and trees. Off in the distance in both directions, she could see two lighthouses. The scenery could not have been more glorious.

Dagney drifted a bit; her line trailed behind. Finally, after what seemed like hours, the tip of the pole bent downward with the distinct pull of a fish! Grabbing the pole, she set the hook. Feeling the extra weight on the line, she knew she had something. The reeling was gentle and easy, with no expected fight of a struggling fish. *Perhaps fangtooth fish don't fight,* she thought. She was in very deep waters, so she reeled a good long time. It was uneventful without a struggle, but there was definitely something on the end of the line. She could feel the weight.

Back home, Muter and Pops had finally stopped staring at each other, and Pops set straight to work. CLICK CLICK CLACK WHRLLLL DZZZZZZT DING RRRIIIIPPPPP CRUMPLE TOSS. After seventeen attempts, Pops had typed a decent letter that looked somewhat professional.

Dear Mayor,

Please don't let Financial Headquarters
build their condominiums at Outhouse
#2. Can you please have them built at
Outhouse #1 instead? Thank you for your
consideration.

Mr. Skully

Just as Pops pulled his final letter from the typewriter, Dagney landed her catch. It was a simultaneous victory.

"Where are the fangs?" Dagney wondered. "Where are the fins, and the scales?"

This was no freak fish from down deep. This looked more like something from her grandmother's china cabinet. Ornate engravings covered the shiny gold surface. Her catch resembled something like an elongated teapot. Having just pulled it up from its watery abode, Dagney started to rub it dry with her dress.

"SOGGY STARFISH!" came an echoing voice from inside. "DO YOU HAVE TO DO THIS NOW?"

The voice startled Dagney, causing her to drop her catch in the hull of the boat.

"CAREFUL!! I just tidied up in here," came the voice again.

Dagney carefully picked up the pot, held it gently in her hands, and continued to wipe it dry with her sleeve.

"Puh-leeze do me a favor and don't rub the lamp anymore!" said the voice.

Still a little frightened, but now more curious, Dagney lifted the lid off the pot to see who was speaking to her. She stuck her face right down to the opening and peered in to see an elderly man standing in the middle of the pot, wearing nothing but a bikini.

"Pardon me!" said the man as he stood with his arms crossed.

Dagney promptly placed the lid back in its place and looked away. "What are you doing in there, mister?"

"First off, I am not a *mister.* I am a *genie*. And secondly, I *was* practicing my belly dancing," said the genie.

"I'm sorry for intruding, Mister Genie." Dagney felt as though she had just walked in on her uncle while he was tending to his bunions. "What's your name?"

"Ernest; my name is Ernest, and according to genie law, you are my master. But may I give you some advice, kid? Don't waste your wishes on expendable goods. Save them for when you really need a good wish and you're all out of options. Take it from an old genie— save me for a rainy day." In a way, Ernest meant it, but really, it was just his way of avoiding work.

"Hello, Ernest, I'm Dagney. Where are you from?" she asked, trying not to lift the lid for another peek.

Ernest pushed the lid up from the inside and motioned Dagney to lean in close. Cupping his hand around his mouth, he hollered in Dagney's ear, "O-HI-O . . . originally."

"Farmland," said Dagney, and she placed the lid back on the pot, shoving Ernest back inside. "I like farms. Your wish is my command, Ernest. I will save you for a rainy day."

Pleased with her catch, Dagney secured the lamp in her bucket, which sat in the hull of the boat, and headed back to the marina. As she came around the south end of San Juan Island and up through Cattle Pass, Shaw Island came into view. As her island grew closer, she could see the long, sandy beach of the campground. With Lopez Island on her starboard and Shaw on her port, she gazed off into the horizon. Scanning the natural beauty of the distant mountains and heavily treed shoreline, she noticed, nestled high in a treetop, an eagle and an ostrich, sitting happily side by side.

Dagney pulled into the marina, docked the boat, grabbed her bucket, and headed up the ramp to the general store. Harold was just leaving the store and about to head home.

"Need a ride, Dagney?" asked Harold.

"Yes, please," answered Dagney. She hopped into the cab of his hay-filled farm truck, her genie lamp safely secured in her bucket.

"Did you hear the news, Mr. Pew?" asked Dagney.

"What news is that, Dagney?"

"It was in the newspaper. Pops read it this morning. The richest man on Earth is going to build condominiums at Outhouse #2," she informed him. "We won't be able to live there much longer."

"Sorry to hear that, Dagney. You know, ever since you moved in there, the property value has increased a lot. I think it's because of your bead strings," he said.

"I think you're right! Pops's job is about to end too, since camping season is almost over. I don't know what we are going to do," said Dagney.

"As your friend and neighbor," said Harold Pew, "I am happy to offer you my outhouse. You and your family can move in there for as long as you need."

"Mr. Pew, we couldn't just—"

Harold interrupted. "Nonsense, Dagney, it's no problem." As he pulled into his driveway, he continued, "I inherited this farm. I'm grateful to have it and I'm happy to share it with friends, especially if they are in need."

"Mr. Pew, you inherited all this?" Dagney scanned the many beautiful acres of forest and pastureland.

"Yes, I did," said Harold. "It used to belong to my great-uncle. He must have passed away, but no one knows for sure what happened to him. One day he just disappeared. He walked out of the house and no one ever saw him again. The police found a note in his handwriting on the doorstep. The note read,

> The time has come. I bequeath my entire estate to my one and only great-nephew, Harold Pew.
>
> Much love,
> Great-Uncle E. Pew

"Anyway, the least I can do is offer to help out my friends and lend you the outhouse." Harold pointed to a small building way out in the middle of his pasture.

Surrounded by blackberries and cobwebs, the outhouse leaned slightly crooked, as though it got tired of holding itself up. Harold had never paid it any attention and had not once gone inside.

"Thanks, Mr. Pew. I'll tell my pops. Can I stop in and look at it on my way home?" Dagney asked.

"Of course, Dagney. Have a peek. I've never stepped foot in there, so it will need a bit of tidying up."

Dagney got out of the truck, grabbed her bucket with the lamp, and headed straight for Harold's outhouse. Although she hadn't caught a fish to bring home to her family, she could bring home the good news about Mr. Pew's generous outhouse offer. She had decided to keep the genie a secret.

The door to the outhouse was cracked open a bit, so Dagney peered in. It scraped across the concrete slab as she pushed it open farther. Clearly, it had not been used in many years. She slipped inside with her bucket in hand. Even though the sun shone in through the skylight, the walls were damp and moldy. Moisture stains had accumulated on the ceiling where rain seeped in. It felt cold and dank. Dagney thought that with a little cleaning it wouldn't be so bad. Perhaps her family could have a new place to live after all. Mounted on the wall behind the sitting area, a bronze sign read **GREAT WALLS WORLD BANK**. Some of the letters looked more worn-out than others. "Why would a bank sign be in this rundown old outhouse?" she asked herself as she climbed up on the bench seat to get a closer look.

What Dagney hadn't noticed, perched high up in the corner, holding perfectly still on a ledge, was a fat gold-colored Persian cat wearing a grimacing scowl. He was not happy with the snooping intruder and watched every move she made. The moment Dagney climbed up on the seat to view the sign, the cat leaped from his perch in an attempt to scare her away. This threw Dagney off balance, causing her to fall sideways into the outhouse receptacle, landing square on her *tuchus*.

Considering where she fell, Dagney expected to be neck-deep in sewage. Instead, she found that she had landed on a large pile of gold coins. Looking around, she was quite surprised to see that she had not fallen into a sewer pit, but rather, what looked to be a vast underground chamber, filled with pots of gold and treasures. Still startled, she collected her bucket and lamp, and wondered how she could get out. It had been quite a drop, and there was no ladder or rope to pull herself out.

A crystal chandelier dimly lit the elegantly furnished room. This was no outhouse like she had ever seen. This was a room built for a king. It was brimming with wealth. However, it did not feel warm and it was not a welcoming space. It was just a very full room, full of very empty treasures. Heads of an elephant, a walrus, and a rhino were mounted on the walls. In one corner stood, what appeared to be, a real-life Sasquatch next to a log, surrounded by native vegetation. This terrified Dagney for a moment, until she realized it was stuffed and mounted like all the others. Dagney needed to get out. She wanted to go home.

In the far corner of this vast, cavernous parlor stood a bed—a canopy-covered cat bed. On the walls around this bed hung many pictures and paintings, which all bore the image of the longhaired

Persian cat that had just scurried from the outhouse. Mounted right over the bed was a larger-than-life-size painting of the cat. In elegant calligraphy, the name "Wiggins" was scrawled across the entire span of the image. It was clear that Wiggins adored his own image and reflection. In addition to all the paintings and photographs of himself, two mirrors hung beside his bed. Another hung on the wall by the gold-weighing scales. Wherever he stood in the parlor, this self-absorbed Wiggins could admire himself from every angle.

Next to the canopy cat bed, Dagney noticed a tunnel. At the entrance to the tunnel stood a large desk with a set of blueprints titled "Pacific Coast Condo Plans." Next to the blueprints sat an untitled manuscript with the words "TOP SECRET" embossed on the cover. She opened the notebook and found a classified report on all species of plants and animals that would be destroyed as a result of the condominium project; mammals, birds, reptiles, insects, fish, and even the whales would be in jeopardy! Then there were the trees: pine, fir, cedar, hemlock, madrona, and maple. The report went on to describe, in great detail, all the destruction this project would cause. Loss of habitat for one species would, in turn, cause loss of another species, and so on. Everything would be replaced with condos, concrete, and parking lots. This was *not* the Outhouse #2 condominium project she had already heard about; this project was much larger. This project was going to cause horrendous destruction and loss of wildlife, all along the entire Pacific coast.

In her dismay and desire to get out of Harold Pew's outhouse, she wandered down the tunnel, hoping it would lead her to an exit. She walked and walked, down the narrow hallway, which seemed

absurdly long. After some time, she could no longer see the room from which she'd left. There were no windows, just dimly lit lamps mounted on the wall every thirty feet or so. Plush carpet lined the center of the walkway, muffling her footsteps. The arched ceiling bore the weight of the earth above her.

Not knowing where the tunnel led, and not seeing an exit, Dagney froze. She considered turning back, but only momentarily, as her desire to escape kept her moving forward. She counted the lamps as she passed, just to keep her mind occupied. On her fifty-second lamp, the texture of the carpet changed and the walls starting closing in. The tunnel was getting smaller. The carpet had turned to bare dirt, and she could no longer see any lamps mounted on the wall up ahead. Instead, she could see a speck of light shining through what looked to be a small opening. It looked like daylight.

As Dagney approached the opening, the dampness of the underground earth permeated the air. She could smell the organic essence of rotting wood and hear the distant sound of birdsong. Cautiously, as she emerged, she glanced around to get an idea of her surroundings. She had walked so far, it felt as though she could be on another island. Surrounded by dense vegetation and tall trees, she was glad to be outside again. On her right, she was pleased to see a wooden structure with a familiar set of stairs—the steps to her very own Outhouse #2. For a moment, this came as a welcome relief, but then she realized she had just come out of the very hole in the tree that Pokkitt had warned her about. Poison ivy! She made her way to the steps as quickly as she could and hoped she had not made contact with the ivy.

Dagney quietly hid the genie lamp in the oven, a place she knew no one would ever look. The next morning when she awoke, she was relieved to see no sign of poison ivy blisters.

CHAPTER 5

RUSTY WRECKAGE

Fourteen days after Pops had mailed his letter to the mayor, he received a reply. By now the days were growing shorter, and the leaves were falling from the maples. It was a drizzly morning in mid-October. Over coffee, Pops first read the daily news headlines. Then, with a lump in his throat, Pops read the letter from the mayor.

Dear Mr. Skully,

I regret to inform you that construction of the condominiums has indeed been set to begin at Outhouse #2 starting in five and a half weeks. A deed of trust has been received by Great Walls World Bank, and a bid has been awarded to Hammer Hacks General Contractor. My apologies for any inconvenience.

Sincerely,
The Mayor

Pops put down his coffee, stood up, and announced, "Pack up your things, we are hitting the road." The background music was sad. Everyone was sad. It was the beginning of the end of Shaw Island.

Earlier that summer, the Skullys had attended the county fair on San Juan Island. It was a wonderful event, with activities and attractions like 4-H livestock, food vendors, pie- and jelly-making competitions, cotton candy, and, of course, the carnival rides. While meandering through the fair, they discovered the Trash-to-Treasures booth. Mounds of discarded items had been piled into various containers dispersed throughout the work area, with tables and tools for everyone to use. Trash-to-Treasures was a live, interactive invention-making playland. Everyone had a good time building gadgets, doohickeys, and thingamajigs out of old junk. The owner of this booth was a connoisseur of welding. He welded sculptures, such as fish, fruit, and flowers, out of unwanted forks and spoons. He also welded cars and campers. A small camper trailer sitting right out in front of the booth caught Pops's eye. It was just the right size for his family, and it was for sale. To show his interest in the trailer, Pops shook the man's hand and asked his name.

"Regarded Rothburger. We wrangle rusty wreckage regularly." (Translation: My name is Rothburger and I collect a lot of junk.)

"Cecil Skully. Sincerely splendid salutations, sir." (Translation: I'm Cecil Skully. Hello, nice to meet you.) (Pops couldn't believe he was speaking like that.)

"Warm welcome. Welded wander wagon while weekend waned." (Translation: Nice to meet you. I built the camper trailer Sunday night.)

"Igniting interest. Ideal imagery. Inquiring into investment." (Translation: I'm interested in the trailer. I like the way it looks. Can I buy it?)

"Palatial proportions! Prepared preposterously palatable. Pleasure." (Translation: It's large enough for your whole family, and it looks like it's just your style. Of course, I'd be glad to sell it to you.)

"Collect call, come curtains." (Translation: I will call you if we have to move out of the outhouse and we need the trailer.)

With that, Pops sealed the deal on his and his family's future. He slipped Rothburger one of Dagney's bead strings as a sign of good faith. The bead string's word was "WELD." Rothburger was now part of the bead-string culture, and he felt it. He felt the magnificent energy the bead string delivered throughout his body. He now had love, respect, and appreciation for all of life and all things good, including those pesky crows that kept stealing shiny objects from his Trash-to-Treasures booth.

* * *

The Skullys tried to make it a happy event, but packing up all the household belongings was a sweet sorrow. The campground had been a lovely place for them, and they had so many fun adventures and met many wonderful people. At the same time, there were untold adventures ahead.

Dagney worried about her bead-string project. Would anybody care about it anymore? She vowed to continue making her bead strings, even while they were living on the road. She could disperse them in random places for people to find. That was important to her, but for now, she had something more important that needed tending to. Quietly, Dagney retrieved the genie lamp from the oven. She had to hide it somewhere safe. Although she didn't know when, her plan was to someday return for it. She had thought about taking it with her but didn't want to risk losing it, or worse, someone else finding it.

Digging a hole in dry sand is not easy; the sand continually collapses in on itself. Dagney discovered this as she dug her hole. The family was loaded in the car and ready to go, but Dagney was busy burying the lamp. The base of the staircase that led down to the beach was her location of choice. The tide never came in that high, and it was an easy landmark to remember. Halfway through her hole digging, she could hear her brother Corey calling for her.

"Dagney, where are you? Dagney, time to go!" Corey yelled out. His voice grew louder as he got closer.

Dagney had to hurry. She didn't want anyone to see her genie lamp, so she quickly threw the lamp in the hole and covered it over. It was only two feet deep, instead of the three feet that she wanted. "On my way," shouted Dagney as she climbed up the flight of stairs.

With everyone loaded, Pops pulled out of the campground and headed to the ferry. Taking one last look back at the wonderful little campground she had grown to love, Dagney noticed a cat sitting on a stump along the edge of the road, tail swishing. She recognized the cat. It was Wiggins from Harold Pew's outhouse. The long, golden fur and razor-sharp scowl was not the last image of the campground she wished to remember.

CHAPTER 6

THE KEEPSAKES

The Skullys were about to start their life on the road. They pulled onto the ferry for the trip to the mainland. As every island passed by, it brought them closer back to "the real world," with people and traffic-filled cities and highways awash in litter and noise. Frustrated from fighting freeway traffic, Pops veered west onto Highway 101. This scenic route spanned from Olympia, the capital of Washington State, and headed north, up and around the beautiful rain forest of the Olympic Peninsula, where black bear, mule deer, and bobcat made their homes, deep in the forest. It is believed that the fabled Sasquatch does as well. The highway begins its descent south, along the Pacific coast, around the small town of Sappho, where women wore plaid and held chainsaw-sculpting competitions. Carving bears and eagles in a tree stump with a chainsaw was the popular form of art in that region.

Being on the road created opportunities for everyone to try new hobbies. Muter tried her hand at extreme ironing. She was able to iron three shirts while surfing a single wave in the Pacific Ocean. Dagney rigged up a table with her pulley for some extreme pic-nicking. She hoisted the picnic table high into a Douglas fir while everyone sat at it, eating hot dogs and potato salad. Everything was extreme. Pops's hobby was extreme water conservation. He made it his goal to survive on only five drops of water a day. That included dish washing, cooking, and washing his socks. He could do it too! They bartered. They traded. They survived. Although everyone was having a wonderful time, Dagney could not get her mind off of the blueprints and top-secret classified report she had seen on Wiggins's desk back in the underground gold vault. Yes, she was sad about the condo project at Outhouse #2, but the Pacific Coast Condominiums project would be far more devastating. She could not imagine the entire coastline torn up. Trees would be cut and replaced by endless rows of condominiums. Pavement, parking lots, strip malls, and gas stations would replace every inch of the rugged, natural wilderness. This ripped at her heart. If only she could do something to stop it.

It was November 11, and it was Marlin's birthday. By now they had made it as far south as Santa Cruz, California. They'd already had many adventures along the way, but the party they'd attended in San Francisco the day prior was the most memorable so far. Although the Skullys were not well educated, they found themselves at a wine-and-cheese party in The Mission, a popular district of San Francisco. These types of parties attracted very smart people. This made Marlin happy. He sat on the floor in the kitchen, eating chunks of salami and cheese that fell from people's crackers. He listened. He heard amazing stories and learned incredible facts. He particularly liked a professor who taught physics at a big university. She talked about neutron particles, atom splitters, and acoustic levitation—downright genius stuff. Most notably, she talked about a new scientific discovery: the neutrino. It was thought to have been discovered that it could travel faster than the speed of light—one billionth of a second faster. This theory would change everything science understood about physics. Pops and Muter had no idea what this meant, so Pops would say things like, "It's impossible for a cow to jump over the moon" and "By the way, the moon is not really made out of cheese."

Muter told the professor that it was her son Marlin's birthday and asked if she had anything that would make a good gift for a physics lover. The professor thought about it for a few moments, then told Muter to follow her to the laboratory down in the basement. A half hour later, Muter came back up carrying two boxes, one slightly larger than the other. Both were wrapped in brightly colored birthday paper, with ribbon tied neatly around and a bow on top. She was pleased with her gifts and knew that Marlin would love them.

Dagney bought party hats, party favors, and a birthday cake so her family could throw a big party for Marlin. Muter brought Marlin's gifts out and set them on the picnic table. "Happy Birthday" was sung, a candle was blown, and they dug into the chocolate cake.

"Open your presents, Marlin!" Muter urged, eager to see how excited he would be with his gifts.

"Yes, open them," echoed Dagney and Corey.

Marlin tore into the first gift. Paper flew everywhere. Lifting the cardboard flap, he peeked inside. At first he thought it was a bowling ball.

"Take it out, Marlin, take it out" exclaimed Muter.

Marlin reached in with both arms, cradled the object, and pulled it out. It wasn't a ball at all; it had a slightly irregular shape.

"Do you like it, Marlin?" asked Muter. "It's a black hole. I got it from the professor last night. She had some extras in her laboratory, so I picked that one just for you."

Marlin was delighted. It was what he had always wanted, and without a doubt, would be a treasured keepsake forever.

"Open the other one, Marlin," begged Muter. She couldn't wait any longer.

"Open! Open! Open!" the family chanted.

Marlin couldn't open it fast enough, so Muter helped. This time when Marlin peeked inside, he knew exactly what it was. It was an oval-shaped ring made out of dust particles and electrons, all swirling in a counterclockwise motion. Marlin pulled it out of the box and admired it. Pops looked at Muter with puzzlement. "What is it?" Pops asked.

Muter explained to him that every black hole has an *event horizon*, which is much like a river current at the point right before you go over the waterfall. It is a very strong force that sucks you in, and no matter how hard you try, you cannot swim out. Pops looked concerned. Leave it to his wife to give the child such a gift.

"Don't worry, Cecil, the professor said it would be fine. As long as the two are not joined, they are physically inactive. And, besides,

they were each from a different specimen, so they do not even fit with one another," she reassured Pops.

The theory was that you could have a black hole, and as long as you had no event horizon, there was no way to fall into the hole. And vice versa: if you had an event horizon, but no black hole, there was nothing for the event horizon to draw you into. All was A-OK and guaranteed safe by the laws of physics. Pops hoped she was right, because things could go sideways real quick if she wasn't. But being a trusting husband, he let Marlin enjoy his amazing new birthday gifts. Carnival music played in the background as they ate more chocolate cake and blew party kazoos.

CHAPTER 7

SPECIAL DELIVERY

Everyone knows that "it's lonely being on the road." This was not the case with the Skullys. They had each other, and they were having the time of their lives. But they did miss their friends back home at the campground. Freedom and adventure was the order of the day, but this sort of lifestyle could not go on indefinitely. Eventually they would run out of money. Pops was careful not to overspend, and Muter kept a tight grip on the cash flow. They never ate out, and they didn't go to movies or places that required entrance fees. They had plenty of fun and entertainment without spending money.

Ultimately, Pops was in search of work, so he regularly checked the help-wanted ads. Although his best prospect for employment was with a vegetable farm, he applied for all types of jobs, and in almost any location, such as The Elephant Sanctuary in Tennessee and a snake-milking factory in Santa Fe, which collected venom from snakes. He applied for a job as a circus clown, a hairdresser, a hot-air balloon pilot, and a wedding planner. But none of these jobs were a good fit. He was a farmer by nature and had grown up in the Midwest, where cornfields covered the entire state. He could imagine himself outside in the open fields with his hands in the dirt. It was in his blood. But for now, all he could do was wait. So he enjoyed every moment he had with his family, on the warm, sunny coast of California.

Parking a car and trailer is never easy when traveling through an inner city. So whenever Pops found a large parking spot, they would often stay there for a little while to get some rest and enjoy the scenery. There was a particularly great spot in the Pacific Grove area of Monterey. It was right on the edge of a waterfront park, where both locals and tourists came to enjoy the natural beauty of the ocean and pine forests. It was their second day there. Pops was on his third drop of water for the day and it was early, so he was concentrating hard on washing dishes. It was shortly after noon, and Corey, Dagney, and Marlin were strolling along the waterfront. Businesses had "OPEN" signs flashing in their windows. The alluring aromas of bacon, fries, and pastries filled the air. The day was in full swing.

Up the road, a postal worker strolled along the sidewalk with her cart, stopping at every address to deliver letters and packages. It was nearing the holiday season, so her cart was overflowing. As she approached the end of the sidewalk, she stopped, picked up a package, had a look around, looked at the Skullys' trailer, looked back at the package, then knocked on the trailer door. Pops opened the door.

"Mr. Skully?" asked the mail carrier.

"Yes, I am Cecil Skully," replied Pops.

"Special-delivery package, sir; sign here please."

"What do you mean 'special-delivery package'? There's no address here," said Pops.

"Says right here, 'Special-delivery package: Mr. Cecil Skully and family. A trailer. Could be anywhere, USA.' Says that right here." She handed Pops a package wrapped in brown paper.

Pops took the package and signed for it. A red "FRAGILE" sticker was taped across the top, so he was careful not to drop it. He set it gently on the table and waited for his kids to return. He hadn't ordered anything, so he didn't know what it could be. When Corey, Dagney, and Marlin returned, he handed over the package and said, "This package was delivered to us. Does anybody know what it could be?" There was no return address. Dagney inspected it carefully, then removed the brown-paper wrapping.

Upon removing the lid of the box, they found Rumble the Bumblebee and his three friends Kaos, Sparks, and Pokkitt, all sitting comfortably on a bed of lettuce (a bit wilted), happily eating. Rumble had missed Marlin and the rest of the Skullys so much that he had himself and his pals shipped down to reunite with them. Marlin scooped up Rumble for a big hug. Everyone cheered and they all celebrated by drinking apple cider vinegar and eating clam chowder. It was a delightfully unexpected reunion! The next day, they were back on the road. The Skullys happily squished together to make room for their new insect passengers.

CHAPTER 8

SLAB CITY

Two days later, the Skullys and company arrived at a small make-shift village in the desert, near the eastern shore of the Salton Sea, in Southern California: Slab City, a rogue encampment full of RVs and broken-down buses, plywood shanties, and blanket forts. Although trash was strewn about in far too many places, it had a beauty of its own. Artists, writers, geologists, archaeologists, teachers, and musicians were drawn to this location as a way to live and express themselves freely and creatively. There were no rules, other than to be respectful of one another. It was the land of the lawless, yet maintained itself in a peaceful and intentional manner.

Slab City was home to Muter's brother, who the kids jokingly referred to as Uncle Chainsmoke. It was just before Hanukkah, but Uncle Chainsmoke didn't celebrate that. He didn't celebrate anything, except his bottle of whiskey, his pack of cigarettes, and the ability to walk around his encampment naked, if he so desired. And he always desired.

"Who needs clothes in the desert sun?" Uncle Chainsmoke would say, more as a statement rather than a question. He did manage to find an old pair of denim cutoffs and a T-shirt for the arrival of his niece and nephews. That was a blessing.

This unusual village did have streets, and people followed the rules of the road, mostly, but electricity and water were a luxury that did not exist in this unofficial community. Garbage trucks did not have routes in that part of the desert either. It was truly off-grid with any sort of services and accommodations. The Oasis Club, a small café that sold coffee and breakfast, used solar panels to collect energy from the sun, so the coffee was always hot and the eggs were cooked. It was a gathering space to discuss the day's events, but mostly just to gossip. There was also a library, open day and night, a hostel for those in need of a bed, and an outdoor nightclub called The Range. The Range was an open space with a raised wooden stage and plenty of seating (mostly in the form of abandoned couches and secondhand chairs), where everyone gathered to enjoy performances such as live music, dancing, and theater, or just to let their hair down. It was the Skullys' first Saturday night at The Range, so Pops went all out and did the mashed potato. Muter put on her heels and did the cha-cha. Uncle Chainsmoke tried the hand jive but quickly had to sit down for coughing too much. Marlin crawled around eating popcorn off the ground and drinking kombucha from stray bottles that were scattered among the many derelict sofas.

Originally, Slab City had been a Marine base, but had long been vacated. There were still slabs of concrete here and there, from buildings that once stood. The shell of a swimming pool now served as a skateboard park and a canvas for murals. Dagney, Pokkitt, and Sparks had found the skate park within minutes of their arrival. Dagney became an instant star that Saturday night. Sparks the Firefly lit up the skate-park arena while Dagney played the banjo and levitated herself with her Ac-Lev (acoustic levitation) boots that she had learned about from the physics professor back in San Francisco. The kids at the skate park were in deep admiration of her "magic" talent, so she made friends instantly.

Wanting a little attention for himself, Pokkitt showed off his knowledge by revealing the scientific explanation behind the Ac-Lev magic. "When she plays the banjo," he said, "the music creates sound waves. The banjo is the 'transducer' and the ground is the 'reflector.' Inside her boots is an antigravity liquid foam that helps reduce the effects of gravity. When the sound waves from the banjo hit the ground, they bounce back and physically push her upward."

This made only a little bit of sense to the kids, but the explanation didn't matter; they were thoroughly impressed with acoustic levitation! Dagney was a celebrity.

As the evening grew late, Dagney, Pokkitt, and Sparks gathered their belongings and headed back to the trailer. One of the local girls had mustered the courage to talk to Dagney and approached just before the trio disappeared into the night. "Hi, I'm Kagney. I want you to have this." She held out a bead string with the word "VIBE" on it.

At once, Dagney recognized it as her own work. She graciously received the bead string and said, "Thank you muchly; my name is Dagney!"

Dagney and Kagney stood in the park, face-to-face, just looking at each other. It felt as if they had already known one another, like long-lost friends.

"Where did you get this?" asked Dagney.

"A friend mailed it to me. I love it, but I want you to have it," Kagney replied.

Dagney thanked Kagney again and put the bead string in her own pocket.

"I volunteer at the library. You should stop by sometime. We have lots of good books," said Kagney.

Dagney nodded bashfully. "I will stop by," she agreed. They said their goodbyes and Dagney blissfully levitated all the way home.

First thing the next morning, Dagney made a bead string for her new friend Kagney. The bead string word was "SLAB." She headed straight to the library, but Kagney was not there. So Dagney asked the librarian for a scrap of paper and a pen and wrote a note:

> Kagney, I hope to see you again sometime.
> —Dagney
>
> P.S. I made a bead string for you.

She left the note and the bead string with the librarian at the checkout desk and hoped Kagney would receive it. Dagney went to the library every day, hoping to find her new friend, but never saw her again.

By now the Skullys had been gone from Shaw Island for about four months. Winter at Slab City kept everyone creatively active and happily engaged with local culture. Marlin and Rumble enjoyed playing hide and seek around the black hole. Muter spent her time at the Oasis Club gossiping and cavorting. The hot spring was a favorite hangout for Dagney. Every day, she, Kaos, and Pokkitt walked there to relax in the large water hole. Along the way they would stop at Vendors Alley, where locals set up mini shops. Blankets were laid on the ground side by side, to display their goods, such as handmade jewelry, knives, leather goods, and semiprecious stones. Dagney often found interesting treasures, and vendors gladly accepted her bead strings as trade. Her favorite acquisition was a petrified mastodon tooth that had been dug up in Florida.

One day after returning home from the hot spring, Dagney saw Pokkitt out behind the trailer with his buddies Kaos and Sparks. He was showing off a ring with a large, bright-blue rock embedded in the center. The rock was an unusual specimen, not native to the local environment. She immediately recognized the ring from Vendors Alley. At dinner, Pokkitt was behaving oddly, so later, right before bed, Dagney asked, "Can I see your ring, Pokkitt?"

"Ring? I don't have a ring," Pokkitt lied.

"What were you showing Kaos and Sparks earlier today?" asked Dagney.

"I'm not sure, Dagney. Maybe it was someone else you saw. I'm not the only mantis here in the desert," offered Pokkit.

Dagney let it go, but later in the night, after everyone was long asleep, Dagney got up and looked in Pokkitt's pile of belongings. Underneath some knitting yarn hid the bright-blue lapis lazuli ring. Dagney returned to her bed and for the first time in her life, realized she had been lied to. *Such chutzpah,* she thought. She did not sleep well that night.

The next day, Pokkitt did not go to the hot spring with Dagney and Kaos. Instead, he slept in late and didn't say a word to Dagney all morning. She tried to forget about it, but she just couldn't. After the hot spring, she made bead strings till noon, then she and Pops met up with Muter at the Oasis Club. Muter was in heavy gossip with some local ladies, so Pops engaged in his "volunteer" work of scattering flour on the floor and emptying Uncle Chainsmoke's ashtrays. Still disturbed by Pokkitt's lie, Dagney sat silently watching the people and wondered how she was going to forgive him. Dreadlocks and hacky sacks, guitars and harmonicas, conga drums and bongo drums, and friendly banter filled the café with a rhythm of its own. However, the happy vibe of the Oasis Club was muted by Dagney's dismay. Suddenly, like the crash of a gong, a loud ring sounded out. The folks at the Oasis Club went silent. Every head turned to look at the source from which this sound came. . . . It rang again.

There, behind the coffee counter, covered in dust, on a small tray made of copper and bamboo, sat a telephone. With its rotary dial and curly cord connected to the receiver, it rang a third time. A sound so unfamiliar to the people of Slab City, they all stared silently at the phone, as though they had just seen a real Sasquatch. A cricket chirped as the barista picked up the phone.

"Hello? . . . Yes . . . He is here . . . One moment please." He set the receiver down, picked up the tray, and walked directly over to Pops. "It's for you."

Pops picked up the receiver as the barista held the tray.

"Cecil Skully speaking," said Pops. "Yes . . . yes . . . I am . . . I can . . . I will . . . OK . . . see you then." He gently placed the phone down on the receiver. As the barista returned the phone to its dusty shelf behind the bar, Pops motioned for Muter and Dagney to follow him home. He walked briskly, with a grin on his face, while Muter and Dagney struggled to keep up.

Pops was never one for theatrics or animation, but the moment he got back to the trailer, he put on Muter's cha-cha heels and started dancing around the campsite. He was celebrating the good news. "I," (cha-cha-cha), "have been chosen," (cha-cha-cha), "to be THEE . . . dirt digger . . . and seed starter," (cha-cha), "for Señor Tomato's Fresh Food Farm. And they are even going to pay me!"

Everyone clapped and cheered and hugged as Pops cha-cha'd around the campsite. This news could not have come at a better time, because by now their money reserves were down low. Very low.

"And the best part is," said Pops as he continued cha-cha-ing around, "we will be moving back to the San Juan Islands!"

The news was unbelievable. The Skullys had come to love the majestic beauty of island life—the mountains, the endless waterways scattered with big islands, small islands, marinas, campgrounds, farms, and parks. The beauty was boundless. The family clapped and cheered even more.

The next day, they pulled in the welcome mat and prepared for the trip back home. Dagney dispersed hundreds of bead strings throughout the village for everyone to find. Then she made one last trip to the library, in search of Kagney. It was Dagney's last chance to find her. Sadly, she wasn't there. Pops hooked up the trailer while Muter said her goodbyes to the ladies at the Oasis Club. Marlin and Rumble played quietly together while Kaos, Sparks, and Pokkitt settled in for the long ride home. It was a beeline trip back. They had fifteen hundred miles to go and three days to get there. They made it in two and a half.

CHAPTER 9

THE MiSSiNG PiECE

The San Juan Islands essentially all looked the same, but each had a personality of its own. The welcoming residents of Orcas Island organized organic co-ops and greeted all with open arms; while the local Lopezians lived lavishly and waved to all who passed by. Many other islands filled the waterways as well, but San Juan Island, which was directly across the bay from Shaw Island, was the main attraction, and that is where Pops's new job would take them and where the Skullys would make their new home. They arrived just before spring.

San Juan Island was a tourist destination. People from all over the world came to enjoy the beauty and recreation of the island offerings. They came for the kayaking, the whale watching, the amazing restaurants, and the national parks. They came to camp, hike, and ride their bicycles around the picturesque perimeter that overlooks the Strait of Juan de Fuca. The Skullys arrived at the start of the busy tourist season in the islands. When the ferries arrived from the mainland, it took half an hour to offload the passengers. The streets were clogged with pedestrians carrying backpacks and pulling luggage. Cars with kayaks strapped to their tops lined up bumper-to-bumper all the way up the main street. Bicyclists, RVs, and vans loaded with tourists filled the town to capacity.

The island was populated with teachers, lawyers, dentists, electricians, hair stylists, and artists. There were two grocery stores, two toy stores, an ice cream parlor, and a candy store. There was even a bowling alley and a skateboard park.

Their new landlord greeted them upon arrival. "Regards, renters! Relax. Ritzy residence ready! Recycle run-down rig." (Translation: Hello, Skullys! Come on in and make yourselves comfortable. Your luxurious new home is all ready for you. Give me the trailer back, in exchange for your rent.)

As it happened, just before leaving Slab City, Pops had responded to a "For Rent" ad he'd seen in the newspaper at the Oasis Club. The ad read, "For Rent. A strawberry. Available immediately." Pops called on this ad right away and was thrilled to find out that the strawberry was still available and Rothburger, the wacky welder, would be their new landlord. They moved in right away. The wood-burning stove kept the place toasty warm. It had a large kitchen with a telephone for Muter to keep in daily contact with the yentas back at the Oasis Club. There was a small library for Marlin, and plenty of space for everyone to spread out and enjoy their hobbies.

The next day was Pops's first day of work. He got up, drank his coffee, ate his herring, and read the newspaper headlines, just like he always did. **GREAT WALLS WORLD BANK AGREES TO FUND MASSIVE PACIFIC COAST CONDO CONSTRUCTION PROJECT.**

Dagney looked up from the floor, where she had been watching Marlin eat his breakfast. This was the project she had seen on the blueprints in the outhouse gold vault, back on Shaw Island! She was immediately overcome with incredible sadness. She had been in the vault and seen the top-secret report. She knew that all the trees would be toppled, mountains would be leveled, and all the wildlife would vanish. She knew that pavement would replace prairies, condos would replace conifers, and shanty shacks disguised as luxury condominiums would stretch the shoreline from north to south. This was tragic news!

Pops was confident and excited about his new job. As he walked into the field office for the first time, he was surprised to see an old familiar face: Harold Pew, from Shaw Island. Harold was working for Señor Tomato, who was a jolly good guy with a keen wit and a sharp desire to grow the best produce in all the land. Señor Tomato managed the entire farm, but because it was so large, he hired a lot of helpers. Pops felt he would be good at his new job. He was a farmer at heart and had corn in his blood. Some of the helpers planted seeds, some were in charge of the watering, some did the weeding, and some did the harvesting. They grew tomatoes, beans, lettuce, strawberries, zucchini, and carrots. Pops was hired as a seed planter, but he did a little of everything; he watered, he weeded, and he harvested.

As time went on, Muter fell back into her usual routine of chatting on the phone. At her feet Marlin played with the pots and pans while eating handfuls of flour from the floor. Dagney spent her time going to the toy store and the bowling alley. She played air hockey and bought candy from the quarter machines. She played games with Corey and built puzzles with Rumble and Kaos (who by now had become regulars of the Skully home). Everyday life on San Juan Island had become routine, monotonous, and easy. Dagney began to realize that when life was easy, her need for creativity faded. She hadn't so much as looked at her beads for quite some time. Her bead-string dream was dying.

Dreams are like seeds. They need nurturing. You can't just plant a seed, water it once, and sit back and wait for it to grow. It needs more. It needs good soil, sunlight, the right amount of water, and daily attention to help it grow into a healthy, mature plant. It is joyous and inspiring to see your seed come to life. Dreams need the same kind of daily attention and care. Dagney's bead-string dream was ignored, so it never matured into its full potential.

Pops, however, was hard at work every day, planting and watering seeds, pulling weeds, removing harmful pests, and helping with the harvests. He loved his job, and his seeds flourished. Harvest after harvest, he saw the food grow from seed to market. And every month he brought home a big paycheck, which bought his family plenty of bagels, with extra cream cheese, and lots of cash for bowling, movies, and ice cream. Life was very comfortable. In fact, it was so comfortable that it had become boring. Everything became predictable. Predictable and boring. Besides the changing of the seasons, Dagney's life remained the same, day after day; a routine of toy store, candy store, bowling alley, and skate park. This should have been fun, but instead got old. Even though San Juan had its own version of the Free Pile, Muter did not find joy in the daily trips there. If she needed something, she would simply go buy it. The magic was gone. They were just another ordinary family with an ordinary life. Dagney's seedling bead-string dream had wilted. While Pops's seeds thrived, Dagney's seed was dead. Then she forgot about it altogether.

One day, after two years of ordinary living on San Juan Island, Dagney was so bored, she had nothing new to do, so she sat in the kitchen and stared at the stove. The stove reminded her of the genie lamp, having once been its hiding spot, and she realized she had not once thought about the lamp since its burial in the sand. In the living room, Marlin was climbing up the sofa to pull down his black hole from the display shelf. It was a quarter to five, and Pops would be home from work soon. He would walk into the strawberry, say, "I'm going to get that clock working tomorrow," then pick up his banjo and play till he fell asleep in the bathroom.

Dagney decided to spend some time with her little brother. She found a book and read to him. "The tallest man that ever lived grew to the height of eight feet eleven inches," Dagney read from the *Guinness Book of World Records*. They both loved extreme oddities. Dagney continued to read, "The largest rubber-band ball in the world weighed nine thousand thirty-two pounds, stood six feet seven inches high, and took four and a half years to build." Although it seemed pointless, Marlin decided he would someday beat that record.

The largest egg on record was laid by an ostrich and tipped the scale at five pounds eleven ounces. That reminded Dagney of Rose Buddy, and she wondered how that flightless feathered fowl was doing over on Shaw. She did feel bad that she hadn't kept her promise of returning Rose Buddy to Sister Hilda. Dagney lingered with memories of Shaw Island for a while. Life was just so ordinary now; she longed for those days when people filled the campground, and smoke from the campfires drifted in the summer night air. Those were the days of bead strings and magic; the good old days of Outhouse #2, which by now was probably torn down and replaced with condominiums.

Suddenly, a RUUUMMBBBLLEEE permeated the strawberry. It shook Dagney out of her daydream. It started low, then like the sound of an engine revving up, elevated in pitch. While Dagney had been reminiscing about her days back on Shaw, Marlin had crawled off. He had come up with a great idea, inspired by the largest rubber-band ball in the world. He took his event horizon down from the display shelf, retrieved the black hole, and started to make his own "largest ball ever." He tugged and pulled at the ring of the event horizon. He was able to get one side wrapped around the black hole, but the hole was too big. The event horizon didn't fit. Marlin crawled to the kitchen, grabbed a potato peeler, and scraped away the perimeter of the hole, just like a potato. Thin layers of black shavings accumulated on the floor. After some reshaping, he tried to wrap the event horizon around the hole again. Still a bit too tight, he took off a few more shavings. This time, like a glove, the event horizon slid up and around the black hole to form a perfect fit. That's when the rumbling began.

Dagney froze in shock as the whirling motion of the event horizon, spinning in a counterclockwise direction, grabbed hold of Marlin and pulled him in and around the black hole. As it spun Marlin closer to the center, like water going down a drain, Dagney tried to grab Marlin to pull him out. But the force was too strong, and the event horizon grabbed hold of her too. Muter and Corey came running when they heard the noise, which grew louder and faster. They, too, were pulled in, as they each tried to save the other. They spun round and round, closer and closer to falling eternally into the black hole. There was no escape.

Pops came home from work just in time to see his entire family spinning deeper into the event horizon. Closer and closer, they were drawn toward the black hole of nothingness. Pops stood there helplessly. He knew if he tried to pull anyone out, he, too, would end up in the hole. Stricken with grief, he could only watch in horror as they fell, one by one, into the eternal abyss. As Dagney was about to go, she cried out, "ROOOOOSE BUUUUUDDYYYYY . . ." And then they were gone. All of them. Gone.

Falling to his knees, Pops wept a river. He cursed himself for letting this tragedy happen. He should've never let Marlin play with toys from a physics laboratory. He knew it was dangerous. And why "Rose Buddy"? What did that mean? Pops wept for an hour and then wept some more. How did this happen? Why would Dagney call out "Rose Buddy" as her final words before getting swallowed up into an eternal abyss of nothingness? He sobbed and sobbed. When he was too exhausted to cry anymore, he noticed the *Guinness Book of World Records* lying open to the page with the ostrich egg. Rose Buddy and the ostrich egg in the book; what did all that mean? It made no sense. Rose Buddy was a piece of a jigsaw puzzle that Pops could not make sense of—the missing piece.

The event horizon continued to rumble and spin. Pops built a barricade around the swirling spectacle and just considered it a major inconvenience in his living space. While mourning the loss of his family for seven days, he thought a lot about his family and Rose Buddy. He remembered the time, long ago, when Dagney had promised to return the ostrich to Sister Hilda. That promise was never kept. Maybe this was his punishment for not holding Dagney to her word. He had failed in his duty as a father. He needed to redeem himself and decided he would fulfill Dagney's promise by returning the ostrich to her rightful owner, Sister Hilda.

The next morning, Pops ate lots of herring and drank six cups of coffee; he knew it was going to be a difficult day. As usual, he read the newspaper headlines out loud to his family that now no longer existed. The day's headlines read: **GREAT WALLS WORLD BANK RELEASES FUNDS FOR PACIFIC COAST CONDOMINIUMS. PROJECT STARTS IN TWO DAYS.** After breakfast, he grabbed a knapsack and filled it with potentially useful rescue items. Having never retrieved an ostrich from a treetop, he packed whatever he thought he might need: rope, scissors, buttons, bucket, boots, socks, markers, needle, thread, glitter glue, . . . and his banjo.

At exactly 11:05 a.m., the ferry pulled into the Shaw Island landing. Pops headed to the general store, where he hitched a ride to the Free Pile. He thanked his driver, then walked the rest of the way to the campground. From Campsite #4, he could see Rose Buddy, happily nestled in the treetop. She was indeed still there. But, before the rescue, Pops had to see if Outhouse #2 still stood. It had been over two years since he'd been in there. As he continued down the campground road, he could see the top of the six-story building nestled among the tall Douglas firs, in the very spot that Outhouse #2 once stood.

He could have never imagined the dreadful sight that infringed on the natural beauty of the campground. The condos were poorly constructed and already starting to deteriorate. Shoddy workmanship was evident. The residents looked equally miserable. The faces and souls of the men and women looked weary and worn-out, just like their homes. This broke Pops's heart. He carried on, past the pitiful sight, with only the memory of what once was.

Pops made his way to the base of the tree where Rose Buddy and Robin the Eagle lived, then opened his knapsack. Pulling out all his supplies, Pops suddenly realized the possibility that Rose Buddy may not want to be rescued. She seemed perfectly content with her eagle companion, and had never complained about her tree-top situation. But Pops had a plan. He sewed two big black buttons to the bottom of the sock. Then he cut and glued a tongue, made  eyelashes with feathers, and finished it off with a little glitter, just for good looks. He now had the most handsome ostrich-head sock puppet Rose Buddy would ever lay eyes on. He placed it on a stick and strapped it to his body. Then he put on Dagney's Ac-Lev boots, slung the bucket over his shoulder, grabbed the banjo, and started playing. He played hard and he played fast. The faster he played, the higher he rose. He picked like he'd never picked before, and eventually levitated himself up two hundred feet, to the top of the tree where the eagle's nest lay. The moment Rose Buddy saw this handsome new arrival peering over the edge of her nest, she swooned in delight and immediately fell deeply in love with the sock-puppet ostrich. The puppet head was so tantalizing that Rose Buddy got up and stepped out of the nest and into the bucket. Once she was in the bucket, Pops slowed the banjo picking, which started the lowering process.

Safely down on solid ground, Pops headed back across the beach to the staircase. Rose Buddy followed close behind, swooning at the sock puppet the entire way. Pleased with himself, Pops was about to follow through with Dagney's promise to return the ostrich to Sister Hilda. Although this wouldn't get him his family back, it was a noble act and gave him a sense of fatherly pride.

As Pops reached the top of the staircase, he dropped all his gear and tossed the sock puppet into the trash can. This was devastating for Rose Buddy. She had just left her eagle companion only to see her new love get tossed out like rubbish. Her heart was broken. She couldn't bear the sadness, so as ostriches are known to do when fearful or sad, she ran back down the stairs to the beach and buried her head deep in the sand. The sadder she felt, the deeper she buried her head. Her heart was so broken that she buried her head two feet deep. She tried to bury it farther, but her beak became wedged into something beneath the sand. She was able to pull her head out of the sand, but the obstructing object was still stuck to her beak. When Pops noticed something stuck to Rose Buddy's face, he quickly ran down the stairs and pulled the object off of her beak. Curious to find out what it was, he started brushing the sand from its exterior. He was startled to hear a voice from within.

"FLOPPIN' FLOUNDER," grumbled the voice.

Not believing that the sound was coming from inside, Pops looked around to see where it might have come from. He continued to brush the sand off, until he could see that it was some sort of elongated teapot.

Obeying the laws of geniehood, Ernest came out of the spout, billowing like smoke until fully manifest in bodily form. He hovered above his lamp. With a deep sigh and little enthusiasm, he choked out, "I am your genie. Your wish is my command."

Pops stood dumbstruck. Was this real? He had heard tales, but never had he seen the likes of this. The genie looked more like a slacker than a shaitan. No silk, no jewels, no vest, no baggy genie pants or ankle bracelet! Indeed, Pops's genie was wearing dirty, worn-out jeans, a long-sleeve T-shirt, a short-brimmed cap, and sandals. He hadn't shaved in a very long time. (Perhaps that was normal for a man genie?)

"My name is Ernest; I am your genie," he mumbled again. "Your wish is my command."

After gathering his wits, Pops held out his hand, gave Ernest a sturdy handshake, and said, "Cecil Skully. Pleased to meet you. My only wish is to get my family back." He told Ernest about his family and how he'd lost them to the black hole. Ernest remembered Dagney from years ago. He was sad to hear about her dreadful fate, so he knew it was time to "genie up" and grant this wish. The "rainy day" had come.

Ernest folded his arms and gave a sharp nod with his head, as genies do. In a flash, Pops found himself back in his home. He, Ernest,

and Rose Buddy stood in the kitchen of the strawberry, next to the black hole, which was surrounded by barricades and caution tape.

"SUPERNOVA, CECIL! This is quite a specimen you have here," exclaimed Ernest as he studied the remarkable space oddity. "You know you're asking me to break all the laws of physics, don't you?"

"You're a genie; that's what you do," said Pops.

"Right," said Ernest, half-heartedly. Ernest had always felt guilty about his failures in genie school. He'd gotten Cs and Ds in most of his courses, and his professors told him that he was an incompetent slacker, which was actually true. So at this point, Ernest wasn't overly confident that he could fulfill his command. As he studied the swirling ring of the event horizon, he waved his arms around and recited some genie chants he'd learned in one of his classes. (Ernest did, in fact, do well in the theatrical courses of genie school; he'd gotten an A minus in genie acting class.) But Pops was not impressed with Ernest's theatrics and was quickly losing faith.

After studying the black hole for a bit longer, Ernest suddenly got an idea. He went out back, behind the strawberry, to find the tool he needed. Prior to attending genie school, Ernest had spent a few years in the town of Sappho, where he mastered his skills at chainsaw carving. He could carve a full-size Sasquatch with incredible detail in just under two hours. Ernest spotted a chainsaw on top of a log pile. Now it was time to combine his genie skills with his carving technique to grant a most difficult wish. He had only one shot at it. If he failed, he, too, would be forever lost in the eternal black hole.

He sharpened every tooth with utmost precision and made sure the gas tank was full. Then he yanked the cord to start the engine.

With the chainsaw loudly buzzing, he walked confidently back to the kitchen, gave Pops a solemn nod, then jumped headfirst into the swirling mass of space-dust particles. He was now in the orbit of no return, but he was ready. As he spun closer to the black hole, he began to carve off the outer layer of its edges. He carved as much and as hard as he could, and by his fifth spin around the hole, he had removed enough blackness to reduce it in size, causing the event horizon to no longer fit snugly around its "host." By now it was just too large to fit, so the event horizon collapsed and fell to the floor, much like Uncle Chainsmoke's denim cutoffs, after he'd lost fifty pounds. Ernest fell to the floor as well.

All the rumbling stopped. Everything went quiet. Pops and Ernest looked at one another for a long while.

"Well, I'll be . . . it worked!" Ernest finally said. He was completely surprised.

"It surely did," agreed Pops.

They waited. They watched. They stared at the hole. Nothing happened. Finally, Pops grabbed the black hole and shook it like a pepper shaker. Out popped Corey, then Marlin, then Dagney and Muter. There they stood, in the strawberry, only a little *fershlugina* and bruised.

Marlin was no longer allowed to play with space toys after that.

CHAPTER 10

THE "WIG" IN THE WIGGINS

What is a wig, but a carpet that lies
Atop a secret the owner despise?

To his very core, Wiggins was greed. Merely a cat, but the color of this Persian feline was a physical reflection of his greatest desire: gold! His long golden fur camouflaged him against the backdrop of his vast piles of gold coins. Although his underground vault on Shaw Island was brimming with huge sums of gold, his appetite for wealth could never be satisfied. The very purpose of this Pacific Coast Condominiums project he was funding was to increase the size of his fortune. He was eager and driven beyond logic to acquire more wealth for himself. The more he loaned out, the more he received back in profit. His grand scheme was to create living spaces out of very cheap material and with very cheap labor and to sell them at a highly inflated price. He had convinced people that this was a good idea by promising the public that their lives would be great, and everyone would have jobs. "Trust me, this is the greatest project in the history of mankind."

Dagney knew all too well the reality of this Great Wall of Condos. But the top-secret report she had seen in the vault was never mentioned in the newspapers. Dagney knew that Wiggins's assurance to the people that "everything would be great" was a big lie. He didn't care how much destruction his project would cause; he had only two things on his mind: money! (the more he had, the more he wanted) and power! (the people would become slaves to him to pay off their debt). His condos were low quality, purposely designed to fall apart almost immediately, so that the owners would have to come to him to borrow more money for all the repairs. More profits for himself. The greed in Wiggins's soul was a starving beast that could never be satisfied. After loaning the money to the developers, Wiggins was just sitting back, waiting for the profits to start rolling in. He sat in his very sad, very lonely little bed, in the corner of his big underground gold vault, just below the outhouse in Harold Pew's pasture. All alone, he waited for his piles of gold to increase in size. All alone, he looked at himself in the mirror. All alone. All alone, that is, except for one other.

In the opposite corner of the room, Wiggins's business partner sat on a chaise lounge next to the stuffed Sasquatch. It was his partner in crime, and his partner in lies and deceit. One generally does not get rich through an honest hard day's work. Not most people, anyway. Wiggins got rich through a series of luck and lies. And now, Wiggins had trust in and loyalty to only one other. And that one other was sitting right there on the chaise lounge, knitting a bright-red pair of golf shorts.

"Are those for you or for me?" asked Wiggins.

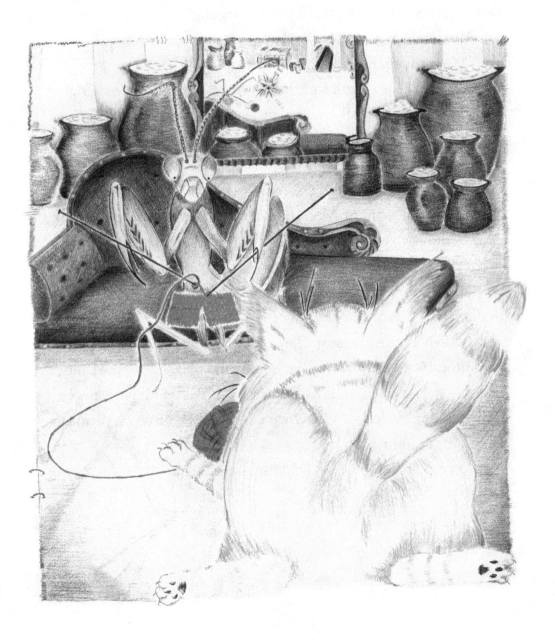

"They are most definitely for you, sir," said Pokkitt. "Our tee time is tomorrow at ten. I can't wait to try out my new set of clubs."

"Terrific! I have a new pair of golf shoes that I need to break in," said Wiggins. "Shall we place a bet on this one?"

"Absolutely, Wiggy," said Pokkitt.

"OK, what are the stakes?" asked Wiggins.

"I'll bet my lapis lazuli ring. It's my finest piece of jewelry. Bright-blue stone with a small amount of pyrite mixed in. It's almost as valuable as diamond," said Pokkitt as he showed Wiggins the brilliant blue rock he had stolen from Vendors Alley, back in Slab City.

Wiggins waged three gold coins. The bet was on.

This was not the Pokkitt that Dagney knew. The truth was, Dagney did not know the real Pokkitt, whose real name was Patrick PcPokkitt. He was a shady hoodlum from Ireland; a pro at snatching up purses from little old ladies. But when he stole a large amount of diamonds and precious gems from the prime minister, he was immediately booked on suspicion, convicted, and given ten years of hard time. He escaped during sentencing and relocated to the United States to start a new life. He had promised to give up his old ways, but he just couldn't help himself. "Once a crook, always a crook" came to be Pokkitt's motto.

"You do amazing work, Pokkitt," said Wiggins. "You're a real professional."

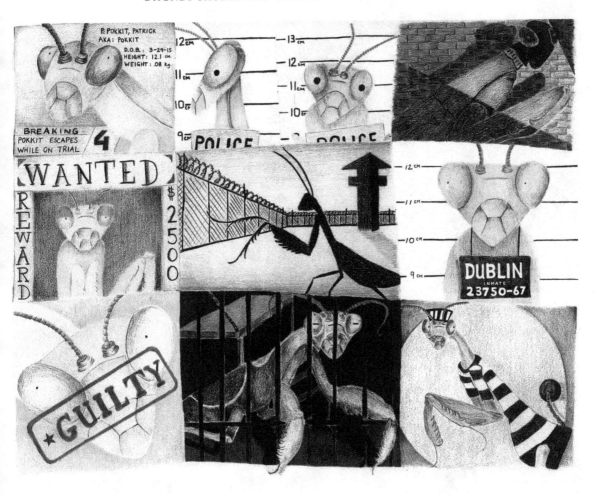

CHAPTER 11

STiCKY FiNGERS

A single tear fell from Pops's eye socket. He was overjoyed. Ernest and Dagney were delighted to see each other once again. "Seems the rainy day has come," said Dagney. Ernest nodded in agreement and gave her a big hug.

The family, having just been recovered from the black hole, insisted on having Ernest stay for dinner. They even served up a dish for Rose Buddy. Apple cider vinegar and clam chowder for everyone! Pops told the family about how sad his life had been without them. He told them about his trip to Shaw Island and how awful the condominiums were. He explained how miserable the people looked, "like worn-out slaves to their expensive condominium lifestyle," and how the newspaper headlines said the Pacific Coast Condominiums project would begin any day now.

Pops went on to explain how he had just rescued Rose Buddy, who was still quite heartbroken. Dagney felt sorry for Rose Buddy, so she made a new ostrich-head sock puppet for her. But as happy as this reunion was, Dagney was worried. The big condominium project would be a disaster she couldn't ignore. There had to be a way to stop the destruction!

To be polite, Ernest had agreed to stay for the meal. He enjoyed hearing the stories and watching the Skullys celebrate, but Ernest had some old business to tend to. He thanked his masters and politely excused himself, promising to be back later that night.

Being a genie did have its advantages. He rolled out his magic carpet and flew to Shaw Island. Landing at the foot of Harold Pew's driveway, he stood there for a while, taking in his surroundings. The driveway cut through the middle of the pasture, with acres of farmland on both sides. Straight up ahead stood a large red barn and a modest little farmhouse. He had not been there in many years, so he was eager to see what had become of it. He walked up the driveway to the front door, knocked, and waited. Soon, Harold opened the door. For a moment, they both stood there, staring at each other.

"As I live and breathe!" cried Harold.

"RAGGEDY ROCKFISH, HAROLD!! Look at you," said Ernest, and they gave each other a big hug.

"We thought you were dead," explained Harold.

"That, I am not," stated Ernest, matter-of-factly.

"Indeed, you are not dead. Bring your living body inside. I just made some carrot cake. I will make us some coffee too." They went inside and Harold boiled water for french-press coffee.

"Harold, you look amazing. All grown up. The last time I saw you, you were just a little sprout. Now you're a full-grown man! I wasn't sure that I would ever be back, but here I am and I'd like to see what you have done with your inheritance."

Harold served the coffee and cake to his great-uncle, who was very eager to find out what Harold had been up to. "I haven't done much, Uncle Ernest; I've lived a quiet life here on the farm. I've got a couple horses I care for, and I visit the sisters over at the monastery. I don't have a wife or any children. . . . I hope I haven't disappointed you. I never expected to see you again. I haven't done much, but I have kept the place up."

After two bites of carrot cake and a sip of coffee, Ernest set his fork down and rested his hands in his lap. He was clearly disappointed and didn't know quite what to say. Finally, with calm vocal restraint, he squeaked out, "The park . . . the water park . . . ?"

"Water park?" asked Harold.

"The water park," said Ernest.

Confused, Harold sat silent for a moment. "What about a water park?"

Ernest brushed the carrot cake crumbs from his beard, wiped his mouth, threw his napkin on the table, and ran outside. Harold followed him to the door. He stood on the porch and watched as his great-uncle ran out into the pasture and headed straight for the rickety, rundown outhouse. Harold had heard stories about his great-uncle being a little wacky, so he figured this is what they meant.

When Ernest got to the outhouse, he circled around with his hand to his ear, listening. He got on his hands and knees and put his ear to the ground. Then he got up and very slowly pushed the door open. Harold stayed on his front porch, watching his great-uncle's odd behavior, not knowing what to make of it. Ernest disappeared into the outhouse for a few moments. When he emerged, he was livid. He stormed back to the house, marched right up to Harold, looked him square in the eye, then dropped his head and cried.

"What's the matter, Uncle Ernest?" asked Harold.

"Didn't you get my letter?" cried Ernest.

"I'm sorry, Uncle Ernest, I don't know what you're talking about."

What nobody knew was that many years back, when Ernest had walked away from the house, he had left not one, but two letters. The sheriff had found the first letter—the one that said he bequeathed his entire estate to his great-nephew Harold Pew. But the sheriff had never seen a second letter, because it had been stolen! Stolen by someone with a long history of bad behavior; someone who made a habit of preying on unsuspecting people. He was, after all, a *preying* mantis. It was in his blood. So Pokkitt had "befriended" Ernest after selling the genie lamp to him and hearing about Ernest's longtime "desire to retire as a genie in bikini at the fangtooth fishy bottom of the salty Salish Sea." While listening to Ernest's stories about genie school, Pokkitt became intrigued by two letters that Ernest held in his hands. He watched with curiosity as Ernest sealed one with wax and stamped it with the official Pew family emblem. The letter was addressed specifically to Harold. Pokkitt paid close attention as Ernest placed both letters strategically where they could be found by the authorities. After Ernest had permanently departed with his new genie-lamp abode, Pokkitt snuck back into Ernest's house and unsealed the waxed, stamped letter. As he read the contents, his eyes grew large.

Pokkitt saw a business opportunity like he'd never seen before, and he shared the letter with his gangly con-artist friend, who, at that time, was a raggedy adolescent kitten. Back then, they called him "Twiggy Wiggy" because he was as scrawny as a twig. But these days, with his long, flowing, golden hair and robust figure, Pokkitt respectfully referred to him as "Wiggins." After Wiggins read the letter, they looked at each other, eyes wide, with much desire in their dark souls. The letter read as such:

My dearest nephew Harold,

I have many dreams, but I am getting old. I do not have enough time left in my life to accomplish them all. I have set out to pursue my lifelong dream of retiring as a genie. I have just one other dream, but I am leaving it for you to pursue, if you choose. I hope that you can make it your dream too.

Harold, in the pit of the outhouse, you will find everything you need to live life comfortably and build this dream. I have left unimaginable riches for you to accomplish this. You see, underneath the acres of pastureland is a large,

deep cavern, which I excavated myself.
My dream is to create an underground
water park. It should have long, curving
water slides, at least five. I imagine there
should be water spouts, wave pools, and
waterfalls. There are enough treasures
in the pit right now to build this water
park and allow free admission for every
child who wants to come play in the park.
I don't know for sure, but I hope to someday return to find that you have made
this dream a reality for yourself, and for
everyone else. It would bring me great joy.
Go to the outhouse located in the middle of the pasture. Inside, you will see I
have already made a sign for the GREAT
FALLS WATER PARK. Just below that is the
pit. Lift the seat cover and look in the pit.
Don't be afraid. The Pew family fortune
is waiting for you there. Build it as you
like, and have fun!

Best wishes,
Great-Uncle E. Pew

Wiggins was a clever guy. He had taken the sign down from the
outhouse and with some strategic rearranging and slight altering

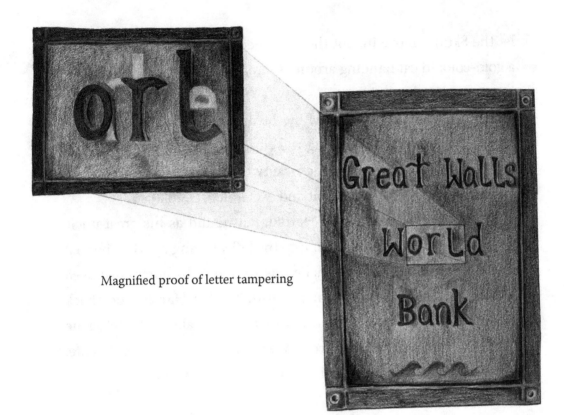

Magnified proof of letter tampering

of letters, he turned GREAT FALLS WATER PARK into GREAT
WALLS WORLD BANK. Meanwhile, Pokkitt had planted poison ivy
at the far end of the tunnel, in back of Outhouse #2, to make certain
that no one would enter from that end.

"Who is responsible for this?" Ernest demanded.

Shaking his head, Harold asked, "Responsible for what, Uncle
Ernest?"

"The outhouse, Harold. Haven't you seen what is going on in the
outhouse?" Ernest demanded to know.

Although rattled himself, Harold tried to calm his uncle. "No.
What is going on in the outhouse? It's just an old shack. I did offer to

let the Skullys move in, but they declined. Every now and then I see a gold-colored cat hanging around there, but that's about it. Nothing is going on in the outhouse."

Ernest grabbed his nephew by the arm and led him to the outhouse. Tripping and stumbling the entire way, Harold, for the very first time, stepped foot into the rickety old shack. Ernest pointed to the sign, then down into the pit and exclaimed, "Look!"

This is awkward, thought Harold, but he did as his great-uncle Ernest asked, and looked down into the hole. Laying eyes on the vast underground cavern of wealth, he was stunned! His horses had been grazing on top of it for years, and he hadn't a clue. Harold stood back and went dizzy with disbelief. Ernest told him about the letter he had left regarding the underground water park, the dream of his life. Harold was overwhelmed with both delight and intrigue.

CHAPTER 12

THE PENDULUM

On her first night out of the black hole, Dagney was so grateful for her rescue that she decided to never again take life for granted. She would never be bored again! First, she would repair the grandfather clock, like she had intended to do years ago. As her Uncle Chainsmoke often said, "If you can build it, you can fix it." She remembered that her grandmother had talked about the clock having some kind of "magic power," so she started on the repair project right after dinner. She studied the clock. Looking at all the gears and moving parts, she quickly diagnosed that the pulley system, which was the key element of the pendulum, had snapped. This was a simple problem to resolve. She had used a pulley system to re-coil the spring on her catapult and to elevate the picnic table for the extreme picnic adventure. She understood how it worked, and now she knew how to fix it.

At precisely 11:11 that night, the pendulum began to swing, the clock began to tick, and the arms began to move. Pleased with her fix, Dagney took out the wooden box filled with beads. She had vowed to start her bead-string project again too. As she opened the lid, something astonishing began to happen. There, in the empty space at the bottom of the poem, the third stanza suddenly emerged in the wood, right before her very eyes.

> *When evil doth about to come*
> *Release the swinging pendulum*
> *And all of those who bear the string*
> *Convene upon what evil bring.*

There is a type of philosophy which states, "The whole is greater than the sum of its parts." With all the gears and other moving parts working, the grandfather clock had become more than just a vessel through which time could be told; the swinging pendulum activated the deeper magic of the bead strings.

Up and down the coast, everyone from Shaw Island to Slab City and beyond felt their bead strings generating this magic. The grandfather clock and the pendulum bead strings were alive once again.

The next morning, promptly at ten, while Wiggins and Pokkitt prepared for their game of golf, the Pacific Coast Condominiums project began. A large fleet of bulldozers and dump trucks flooded the forest, starting in Sequoia National Park. Tobacco-chewing men, carrying chainsaws and wearing hard hats and steel-toe boots, started up their diesel engines. Excavators and logging trucks arrived to load and haul away the massive, ancient trees. The bulldozing of the magnificent redwood forest was about to begin. The first tree to be removed was a giant sequoia. Wiggins had to loan out extra money to ensure the permit for the felling of that tree. It was the largest living tree on Earth, standing 275 feet tall, with a trunk circumference of 102 feet. They called it the General Sherman, and it was estimated to be around 2,700 years old. Some of the other trees were a little older, but most of them were around two thousand years old. That didn't matter. They were all coming down. The felling of the Sequoia National Park was only the beginning. The entire Pacific coast was to be bulldozed.

The chainsaw blade was six feet long. Every tooth on the blade had been precisely sharpened. It took two men to handle this saw, one on each end. The men fired up the saw. Smoke billowed from the exhaust. As the blade of the saw was about to make contact with the thirty-six-foot base of the General Sherman, the lead foreman of the project noticed a mass of people off in the distance, and they were quickly approaching. All the loggers stopped to see what was happening. Then they noticed a mass of people coming from the other direction as well. It, too, grew larger and closer. Then a third, and then a fourth mass of people arrived. Soon, the fleet of loggers was entirely surrounded by a swarming mass of bead-string people who had felt the urgent call for help from the pendulum motion of the grandfather clock. An army of bead-string people had arrived to save the precious environment all along the coast. There were thousands of them. They swarmed the forest and surrounded the trees. There were so many bead-string people, that they created a human barricade, hundreds of people deep, around the General Sherman. The loggers could not cut down the tree. The General Sherman was safe, for now.

CHAPTER 13

A CLOG IN THE LOO

If Wiggins wasn't such an elusive cat, it would be easy to catch him and hold him accountable for the theft and destruction he was about to create. But he *was* a cat, and cats are swift. Catching Wiggins was going to be a challenge. But cats also have certain habits, inherent to their nature. They are hunters, and they love to hunt birds. Being a bird, Rose Buddy instinctively knew what she needed to do. She understood Dagney's pendulum-bead-string call for help, and she was willing to put her life on the line for the cause. It was a personal choice, and she made it willingly and with compassion for all of her fellow feathered friends. She told Dagney her plan. Not knowing what else to do, Dagney agreed it was a good idea. She also knew that it would probably be the end of Rose Buddy.

On the eighteenth hole, Wiggins set his ball on the tee. The sun was shining, the birds were singing, and with only one hole left,

Wiggins bantered with Pokkitt. "I'm really going to enjoy that nice blue lapis lazuli ring I'm about to win," said Wiggins.

Pokkitt bantered back, "Game's not over yet, Piggy Wiggy. I sense you're about to choke."

"Face it, Pokkitt, I'll win. You'll lose and I'll win. I always win. You always lose, and I always win, and that is how it always is," boasted Wiggins, as he took some practice swings.

"Hurry up and hit the ball. Let's just get this game over. I'm starving," pleaded Pokkitt.

"Me too," said Wiggins, and with one stroke of the club, he landed the ball on the green. It bounced a couple times then rolled with a slight curve before dropping into the hole. "Sorry for your loss," he taunted. "Hole in one!"

"Bravo, Wiggins; I'd rather lose to you than anyone," said Pokkitt as they packed up their clubs. They shook hands and headed home. Wiggins admired his new ring all the way back.

The previous few days, Wiggins had been keeping an eye on a fat songbird that had been flitting about the wisteria vine near the foot of Harold's driveway. He was hoping today would be the day to feast on the little dumpling. His stomach had been empty just a little too long, and he yearned to stuff it full of chickadee. His mouth was watering and he couldn't wait to sink his teeth into it. As they approached the wisteria, Wiggins was in for the surprise of his life. Lying in the ditch next to the edge of the vine was the biggest bird he had ever seen, and it looked like an easy catch. His eyes grew large as he hunkered down to sneak up on his prey. He didn't like to go hungry, not for one moment, so he moved with stealthy precaution.

When the time was just right, Wiggins pounced. He'd never tasted ostrich before, but he knew she would be delicious!

Wiggins dragged his bird across the pasture and somehow got it through the outhouse door. He planned on stuffing it into his underground vault. It was not an easy task. This bird was big! Wiggins was exhausted, but determined to get it into his lair, where he could enjoy it without the threat of an eagle stealing it away. The head and neck went first. That part was easy. Then Wiggins jumped into the pit, and attempted to pull the rest of the body in after him.

What Wiggins had not anticipated was the difference in size between the entrance hole and this incredibly large bird. Wiggins may have been an excellent con artist and financial guru, but he had no common sense. Pulling Rose Buddy through that hole was like trying to thread a rope through the eye of a needle. Rose Buddy clogged the hole like a cork in a wine bottle, leaving Wiggins trapped on the inside.

Perhaps, thought Wiggins, *I can push him in from the top.*

Since the exit hole was clogged with Rose Buddy, he ran down the long, dimly lit tunnel that exited where Outhouse #2 once stood. (It remained exactly the same as when Dagney had escaped through it after falling into the vault a few years back. Poison ivy and all.) As the carpet turned to bare soil, and damp, organic earth replaced the lamp-lined tunnel, Wiggins could see daylight up ahead. When he reached the opening of the tunnel, he leaped out as far as he could to avoid the poison ivy. Scurrying, he found himself entangled in a mesh of netting attached to a metal pole. Ernest held on tightly to the pole while Dagney cinched the net.

"It's him, Ernest! It's Wiggins! Don't let him get away!" implored Dagney.

They had, indeed, captured Wiggins, the scandalous mastermind behind the Great Wall of Condominiums.

It took three of them—Dagney, Ernest, and Harold—to dislodge Rose Buddy from the hole. They had successfully unclogged the loo, and, remarkably, Rose Buddy had suffered but a small puncture wound, and a few frazzled feathers. Wiggins was turned over to the sheriff, along with Ernest's letter to Harold that had been found under Wiggins's mattress. That would prove to be the most important piece of evidence at Wiggins's trial, along with the top-secret documents regarding the environmental disaster that would be created should the project proceed. Wiggins had thought those documents would never be found, but Harold, Ernest, Dagney, and the sheriff had found them all.

CHAPTER 14

TELL IT TO THE JUDGE

The Pacific Coast Scandal was the trial of the decade. The bead-string people who saved the General Sherman were all there, along with the contractors who had been hired for the job. Thousands of people who had been bamboozled filled the courthouse lawn for the duration of the trial. Ernest, Harold, and the Skullys all had front-row seats in the courtroom. After three days of solid testimony, the judge read the verdict: *guilty as charged!* She struck her gavel as the entire crowd exploded in cheers and celebration. Wiggins was shackled by two guards and made to remain seated for the sentencing. After five minutes of cheering and hugging, the judge returned to the courtroom.

"Silence! Silence in the court!" proclaimed the bailiff. "It is now time to read the sentencing."

The crowd quickly fell silent as they awaited the judge's sentencing.

"Mr. Wiggins," said the judge, "you are a thief and a fraud. You have lied and misled many people. I can honestly say that I am thankful that you were caught before any permanent damage happened. We cherish the beauty of our great planet. Your fraudulent project, spawned from theft and greed, is a deed worthy of the harshest punishment."

The crowd cheered wildly.

"Therefore," the judge continued, "I am sentencing you to the maximum: twenty years in prison, without the possibility of parole."

The crowd roared even more.

"And . . . ," said the judge, "you will return all of the money, including all profits you have wrongfully collected, to the rightful owners, Ernest the genie and his great-nephew Harold Pew. Guards, take him away! Court is adjourned."

The guards cuffed Wiggins and led him out of the courtroom. As everyone hugged and congratulated one another, Ernest pulled Dagney aside. No one noticed as he whispered something in her ear. With a grin, Dagney gave Ernest a wink and a nod.

Suddenly the room filled with the sound of music. Dagney had silenced the crowd with her banjo. All eyes landed on her. When she had their full attention, she jumped up on her chair and announced, "For all the wickedness in one man, there is ten times the goodness in another! There is much goodness here today, and goodness deserves more goodness. For those of you who fell victim to Wiggins's trail of deceit, you shall not go home with nothing. Gather up all your tools and machinery; we have a job for you!" Then she turned to Ernest and announced, "I wish for the greatest water park on Earth!"

Delighted, and with the biggest smile and brightest eyes, Ernest replied, "Your wish is my command!"

Dagney could not have been happier. The entire West Coast was saved from Wiggins's condo catastrophe. The construction workers had a wonderful time building the Great Falls Water Park down in the underground vault in the middle of Harold Pew's pasture on beautiful Shaw Island, just as Great-Uncle Ernest had always dreamed. Harold enjoyed watching his horses graze the pasture, while children from all over the world came to play at the underground water park.

Meanwhile, Inmate 186433 peeled potatoes in his black-and-white striped jumpsuit at the Washington State Penitentiary in Walla Walla. The schmuck he was.

CHAPTER 15

THE PROMISE

A promise is a promise and the time had come. Dagney and Rose Buddy meandered down the long driveway, past the Highland cattle and the llamas. Storage sheds filled with garden tools, barns stacked high with hay, and sporadic greenhouses growing rhubarb and kale were scattered throughout the property. At the end of the driveway stood the chapel and living quarters for Our Lady of the Rock Benedictine nuns. Dagney saw no one as they made their way through the property. She was sad to be leaving Rose Buddy behind, but she understood that the ostrich didn't belong to her. She knew that Sister Hilda would be happy to finally get her helpful farmhand back. From a distance, Dagney heard the faint sound of singing.

Following the sound, she headed toward a garage, which peeked out from behind the chapel. In the garage, mounted slightly up on a jack, a pair of legs wearing faded denim jeans with rips at the knees protruded from under a bright-orange 1974 Volkswagen Bug. Underneath the Volkswagen, lying on the concrete floor, a mechanic whistled and sang.

"Hello?" beckoned Dagney, as she approached the singing mechanic in hopes of getting help finding Sister Hilda.

"Could you hand me that socket wrench?" asked the voice from under the car.

"Sure," said Dagney as she picked up the wrench.

An arm reached out from under the car, palm up, waiting for the wrench. Wrapped around the wrist of the Volkswagen mechanic was a bead string. Dagney recognized this one immediately. She recognized the colors and the special pattern that she had made for a certain someone. The bead-string word was "SLAB." She had thought she would never see that bead string again, but there it was, hanging comfortably around the wrist of the young mechanic at Our Lady Benedictine Monastery. *Promises are always worth keeping,* noted Dagney. She handed the mechanic the wrench along with her own bead string with the word "VIBE." Moments later, a head popped out from under the orange vehicle. It was indeed *her,* Kagney from Slab City. She had come to visit her grandmother, Sister Hilda. So in keeping her promise, Dagney was reunited with a friend she had thought she'd never see again.

That was, indeed, the power of the bead string. Kagney climbed out from under the car as she hurried to embrace her friend. As they hugged each other, Sister Hilda sauntered into the garage where she found Kagney and Dagney in the midst of their happy reunion, while Rose Buddy stood there quietly.

"There ought to be a word," said Dagney, "that means happy and sad at the same time." Dagney was indeed sad to be leaving Rose Buddy behind. But Rose Buddy only felt the sad.

"Bittersweet," said Sister Hilda.

Dagney turned to see Sister Hilda standing there next to Rose Buddy.

"Bittersweet?" asked Dagney.

"The word for being happy and sad at the same time. It's nice to see you again Dagney, but why are you sad?" asked Sister Hilda.

Dagney hung her head. "I've come to return your ostrich as I promised several years ago," she replied.

"Dagney, I think Rose Buddy ought to go where Rose Buddy wants to go," insisted Sister Hilda.

Surprised by Sister Hilda's comment, Dagney pulled the sock puppet from her pocket, put it on her arm, and Rose Buddy fell in love with it all over again. She was free to choose.

ABOUT THE AUTHOR

Sarena Schumacher grew up in Bremerton, Washington, and attended film school at Seattle Central College. Her inspiration for the Skully world began after she moved to Orcas Island and began seasonal work as a park aide at Shaw County Park. During that time, she made bead strings and suspended them in the park's outhouse for campers to take. After many people had asked her who was making the bead strings, Schumacher invented the Skully family and installed their likeness in the outhouse so that visitors could meet the creators of the bead strings themselves. *Dagney Skully and the Pendulum Bead Strings* is her first book and is based on real events. Schumacher lives on a tranquil thirty-acre property with her three tiny dogs and her farm dog, Jack. San Juan Island is her home.

CPSIA information can be obtained
at www.ICGtesting.com
Printed in the USA
FSHW022356160519
58215FS